MOVIE

IN

A

BOOK

THE

BLUE HOSTAGE

707

by

TENI ABEGUNDE

CATAPHRASE MIAB
WWW.CATAPHRASE.COM

AUTHOR'S SIGNATURE PAGE

THREE CONFUSED DWAFTS AND THE MYSTERY
MAN IN THE SHADOWS

"The world is big, yet the world is not enough."
"It's a small world, but we can't lift it up."
"Behold that huge figure in the shadow.
It seems like a dreamer."
"Perhaps he slept to avoid the problems in his boring life."
"But now he has awoken inside the world on his shoulder."
"The path he chose led him to a strange land."
"Often, fear, the invisible enemy, paid him a visit."
"He doesn't flinch. He must be from the land of the brave."
"He would shed blood before shedding a tear."
"Yup, his tears are thicker than blood."
"He traded the pleasure of life for a rifle."
"Death is his strength. Life is his weakness."
"He abandoned his alienable rights and, with honor, put on a
selfless sacrifice."
"Call him day or night, rain or fire. He's always ready."
"Fearless yet cautious of the path he's threading."
"He'll die before he quits."
"He's the Christ."
"Nay, he's not the Christ. He's a sorcerer."
"He doesn't look like a sorcerer. He's a knight."
"I think he's a ghost."
"Yea, I agree. He must be a ghost."
"Nay, he's not a sorcerer, a knight, or a ghost. Not even the
Christ."
"So, who is he?"
"He's a soldier, an American soldier.

In memory of my dad and every Marine officers who lost their lives in battle.

V11/CP1245-1100000913
Cataphrase MIAB
Paperback Edition:
ISBN: 978-0-9916306-7-7
09-13-03-10-01-02-18

0793—V887—The blue hostage/Cp-2

PRINTED IN THE UNITED STATES OF AMERICA

Cataphrase A

Cataphrase B

Cataphrase C

Cataphrase D

Cataphrase E

Cataphrase F

Cataphrase A

"I hate to say it, but it's the truth. Failure and success don't have a secret. If you fail or you become successful: you're either stupid, you're lucky, or you're damn smart."
—Teni A.

Scene 1

[January 20, 2019, Inauguration Day at the US capital]

Hundreds of thousands of people had gathered at the west front of the United States Capitol to witness the swearing-in ceremony.

Chief Justice Barry Cooper was administering the oath of office to me, Neil Bull.

Cooper: "Mr. Bull, please raise your right hand and say after me, 'I, Neil Kenneth Bull, do solemnly swear that I will faithfully execute the Office of President of the United States.'"

Me: "I, Neil Kenneth Bull, do solemnly swear that I will faithfully execute the Office of President of the United States."

Cooper: "And will, to the best of my ability, pre-serve, protect, and defend the Constitution of the United States."

Me: "And will, to the best of my ability, preserve, protect, and defend the Constitution of the United State."

Cooper: "So help me God."

Me: "So help me God."

Cooper: "Congratulations, Mr. President."

Me: "Thank you."

We shook hands.

[Scene 2]

[♫♫. Twenty-one-gun salute…♫]

[Scene 3]

My journey to the White house didn't start the day I was sworn in as president. Not even the year before. The journey started twenty-five years before my inauguration.

There're three categories of people in the world: the rich, the poor, and the myths. The poor and the rich people have something in common. Poor people have time in abundance, but they lack money, while rich people have money in abundance, but they lack time. For this reason, poor people can afford to wait eleven months for the price of a tuxedo to come down before they buy it. Rich people don't have much time, so they'll pay more than the tux is worth instead of waiting till Black Friday.

The last category of people is the myths. They don't have time, and they don't have money. That was the kind of person I used to be when I was younger. I was a myth. I didn't have much time, and of course, I was broke as hell.

Employment is when the poor and the rich people trade time and money. I'm neither one of them, so I had no job either.

After I graduated from high school, I stayed home for two years doing nothing. I knew I wouldn't spend all my life working out and watching TV, which is what I did often. I had to do something with my life. I couldn't sing, I couldn't play football, and I was unemployed; thus, I couldn't afford going to college.

[Scene 4]

The week following my twenty-third birthday, I joined the Marine Corps. There, they didn't ask for time or money. All they demanded from me was loyalty, dedication, and obedience. The Marine boot camp was a perfect escape for a myth.

The Marine Corps recruit training is twelve weeks. I completed mine in eleven weeks and immediately enlisted for special ops training. My strength and endurance were so exceptional that three years after my Marine Corps graduation, I became the first person in the history of the United States to become qualified in all three special operations forces.

[Scene 5]

I was deployed several times during my first three years. After four years, I was promoted to the rank of captain.

The day I was going to receive my insignia, I ran into Mathew, a high school friend. He was also a Marine Scout-Sniper.

In high school, we competed in every sport, including boxing and football. He's a foot taller than me, yet somehow, I defeated him in every competition. When we met again in the Marine Corps, he was assigned as a spotter in my regiment. We trained together for two weeks and immediately reignited our friendship.

[Scene 6]

Around 7:35, the evening of August 9, 1995, It was as if all hell had broken loose at the football stadium adjacent to my house. I peeped through my room window and saw a helicopter landing on the football field. Three uniformed soldiers came out of the helicopter and sprinted towards my house like runaway slaves. Both were about my height, six foot eleven. Before I could put on my shirt, there was a knock on my door.

Officer (at my front door): "Captain Bull, this is the United States Marine Corps. Open the door."

[Scene 7]

I had a concealed Beretta M9 on my waist as I

approached the front door.

[Scene 8]

One of the Marine Corps officers at the door started speaking the moment I opened it.

Officer: "CAPTAIN NEIL KENNET BULL, BADGE NUMBER 76333-88, SPECIAL DIVISION BRAVO, SEAL C4001, RANGER B0001, BERET GM7228. CODE: RED COBRAL, EAGLE ONE."

That was all he needed to say. I was on the helicopter the moment he mentioned Eagle One.

There're only three groups of people in the world who knows what that entire call code means: an officer in any of the special ops divisions, the United States major generals, and the United States president.

My military ID number was 76333-88. The branch of the military I belong to was 88. SEAL C4001, Ranger B0001, and Beret GM7228, in short, meant they knew who the fuck I was. Red Cobra meant America or an American was in danger. Eagle One meant the president of the United States had called on the Marine Corps and they had direct orders to bring me in dead or alive.

Something had happened. I didn't know the nature of the situation, and I didn't ask them. Even if I had, none of them would have talked. Their assignment was to bring me in, period. I sat back throughout the helicopter trip and prepared my mind for the worst.

When the helicopter touched down at Blount Island Command in Florida, I was led to the colonel's office.

[Scene 9]

[Inside the colonel's office]

I stood in front of the colonel after a brief salute. He was reading my military record.

Colonel: "Neil Kenneth Bull. Born in Pennsylvania, July 8, 1970. Left-handed. Marital status: single. High school: Westbrook. No college. Joined Marine Corps in 1991. Combat experience: seven deployments. Shot on target is rated accurate. Speed is rated impeccable. Endurance is rated immaculate. Stealth is rated invincible. Fear is rated sub-zero. Good at knife catching.

"Foot path sniffing measured at 0.7 O.U.

Underwater breath holding: five minutes. Weapon of choice: Beretta M9. First soldier to qualify for all United States special operations forces. Successfully passed Ranger training in five weeks, Navy SEAL training in seven weeks, and Green Beret training in seven weeks. Seventeen thousand shots on target and still counting. Sixty-seven competitions, no loss. *Soldier, who the hell are you?*"

Me: "Neil Kenneth Bull, sir, United States Marine."

Colonel: "I know, but how come I have never heard about you?"

Me: "I'm not as famous as you, sir."

Colonel: "Well, you're about to be. I ordered those gentlemen to pick you up because your name is listed first in the classified mission data. Neil, you've got less than an hour to put on your gear. The mission we need you to execute is classified, and it must remain so until the mission is over.

Lieutenant Sam will brief you on your assignment when you get on board. With such an outstanding record, I don't expect anything less than perfection. America is counting on you, Neil."

Me: "I'll try my best, sir."

Colonel: "Good luck."

[Scene 10]

Most assignments carried out by special ops are classified. Yet a soldier can predict the nature of his mission ahead based on the gear he or she is instructed to wear.

One pack of Marine M10 gear contains enough weapons, med kits, food, and drink to last two soldiers in a desert for a month. When I was instructed to equip the M10, I knew I was heading straight for hell.

[Scene 11]

As usual, when I'm about to do something audacious, I'll say the Bull's prayer: "The lord is my shepherd. I shall not want. . ."

[Scene 12]

The military AC-130 plane transporting me

departed **Blount Island Command** around 10pm. The plane didn't have passenger windows, and I didn't look at my watch; hence, I couldn't tell you how long we traveled or what direction the plane went. I believe I received my briefing one hour into the flight.

[Scene 13]

[Inside the AC-130 military airplane]

Lieutenant Sam entered the deployment section, where I was seated.

Lieutenant Sam: "Captain."

Me: "Yes, sir."

We shook hands.

Lieutenant Sam: "I'm Lieutenant Samuel. You don't have to introduce yourself. I know everything about you that I need to know.

"In twenty-five minutes, this plane will be over Cuban territory. Here is your mission map. That area circled on the map is where you will be conducting surveillance. The area circled in green is where we believe Catherine is being held captive."

Me: "Catherine? The tourist girl that went missing in Cuba?"

Lieutenant Sam: "Yeah, that's why you're here. I'm sure you've seen her face several times on the news. Here's her picture. She has a tattoo on her left leg: a flower, rose or something. I'm not sure."

Me: "Is this a rescue operation?"

Lieutenant Sam: "Yes, but not for you. Your assignment is to conduct surveillance and gather information ahead of the SEAL team that will carry out the rescue operation.

"You shouldn't encounter any threat in the Zapata Forest, where you will be landing. According to our satellite surveillance, no one has set foot in that forest in a long time."

Me: "If I do?"

Lieutenant Sam: "Captain, you know what to do.

Here are your radio codes for communication. Use them when you talk on the radio. Green Apple is the code name for the rescue mission. Green Apple refers to Catherine. Your code name is Eve. The SEAL team that will carry out the rescue operation is code named Gabriel."

Me: "When will the rescue operation happen?"

Lieutenant Sam: "I'm afraid, Captain, that information is also classified. However, we will inform you ahead of the mission. Is there anything else you want to know before you jump out of this plane?"

Me: "The lord is my shepherd. I shall not want."

The plane rear door opened.

Lieutenant Sam: "*Alright, Captain, get behind the strap . . . Three seconds to go, counting down . . . Stand by, at my command. . . GO.*"

[Scene 14]

I plunged out of the plane like a dart. All I saw when I dove towards the earth was pitch darkness.

My night vision sprung on after five seconds, followed by my parachute.

[Scene 15]

My landing zone was a forest near the southeast of Zapata Swamp, overlooking a small village on flat terrain. Other than cattle grazing and a few kids playing, which I observed about a quarter of a mile away through my night vision telescope, there was no activity close to the forest. I selected a green ghillie suit to wear because it resembled the background color of the forest.

Throughout the night, I scanned the houses in the village through my rifle scope, paying close attention to the ones with the most activity.

The villagers were going about their daily lives. Quite a few people were outside their houses. Three kids were running around a hut, and a lady in a white dress was braiding another woman's hair, while most of the remaining villagers were cooking. The night passed, and I didn't observe anything unusual.

[Scene 16]

In the early morning, I took a short water break and

relaxed my neck on my backpack. I was about to open a can of sardines when I heard the sound of gunshots echoing from some distance away. I got back on my scope, and what I saw happening in the village was horrendous.

[Scene 17]

A group of armed men had just carried out a massacre. The lifeless bodies of women and children littered the ground. I watched in horror as the bad guys took turns ravishing and killing young women.

The sweat on my skin boiled. I had enough ammunition to take out the bad guys, but my assignment was clear: conduct surveillance, not save the world.

[Scene 18]

I glanced at Catherine's picture and turned my scope to the building where we believed she was being held.

[Scene 19]

I saw four armed men bringing some people out of

the building. None of them resembled Catherine. For a moment, the killing and beating stopped. A blue van pulled up near a tree. Two armed men came out of the van with two female captives. They led the two captives towards the building I was looking at through my scope.

The hands of both captives were tied, and their faces were covered with brown burlap sacks. The tattoo I saw on the left leg of one of the captives was unmistakable: it resembled Catherine's, but I didn't have a positive ID on the lady's face.

[Scene 20]

I relayed the information back to the closest United States Navy ship in the Caribbean Sea.

[Coded radio call]

Me: "Command, this is Eve. Do you copy?"

Command: "I copy, Eve. Go ahead."

Me: "A figure here resembles Green Apple."

Command: "Hundred percent Green Apple?"

Me: "Negative. Sixty percent Green Apple."

Command: "Copied. Gabriel will rain tomorrow. Refer to line seven of your RC."

Me: "Roger that. Line seven is acknowledged."

Gabriel would arrive at 10pm. That was the code on line seven in my RC.

[Scene 21]

When I got back on my scope, I saw two of four isolated bad guys drinking and tossing the two female captives around. It was hard watching how they treated the two ladies. Despite this, I kept my eyes on the lady I suspected was Catherine.

One of the four armed men walked across the yard and took the sacks off both female captives. Their backs were turned towards me, yet I kept my scope on the lady with the tattoo. One punch from the bad guy was what turned her face around. The ID was positive. The female captive with the tattoo was Catherine.

[Scene 22]

The second radio call went out immediately.

Me: "Command, this is Eve. Do you copy?"

Command: "Eve, I copy."

Me: "I have positive ID on Green Apple. I repeat, Green Apple is one hundred percent positive."

Command: "Roger that, Eve. Command is changing plan. Gabriel will rain today. Refer to line seven of your RC."

Me: "Line seven acknowledged."

The rescue operation was scheduled for 10 pm that night, twelve hours away. I pinned my scope on Catherine and continued to observe what was happening around her.

[Scene 23]

Catherine and the other lady were lying on the ground, with four armed men close by, drinking.

[Scene 24]

The other nine captors were on the other side of a building, about five to six yards away from Catherine. The remaining villagers were tied up either outside or inside the buildings.

[Scene 25]

Two of the four isolated bad guys grabbed Catherine and the other lady, one each, dragging them inside the building.

From the reaction on their faces, coupled with what I had seen them do earlier, I had no doubts about what they were about to do to Catherine and the other lady.

[Scene 26]

I stood up from my sniping position. The distance from where I stood to the village was approximately half a mile. That was less than a five-minute run if I sprinted at high speed. It was either then or never. I could either sit there and watch the bad guys rape Catherine or go in and carry out the rescue operation.

The third radio call went out.

Me: "Eve to Command."

Command: "Eve, go ahead."

Me: "There's a problem."

Command: "Eve, what's the problem?"

Me: "Green Apple is in trouble. The thunder is about to strike."

Command: "Roger that, Eve, I can reduce line seven to a quarter."

Me: "Still won't help. It has to happen now, or it will end before it starts."

Command: "Roger that. How many thunders can you confirm?"

Me: "Ten, eleven maybe."

Command: "Eve, what are your chances of success if you're asked to pluck Green Apple?"

Me: "There are four thunders around Green Apple. I can take them out silently and then proceed to the building and secure Green Apple. I'll silence the rest as they approach Green Apple."

Command: "Your plan sounds great, Eve, but that approach is too risky. However, refer to line nine of your RC. Gabriel is on the way."

As an alternative, Eve was to take necessary action if Green Apple was in a life-threatening situation. That was code nine of my RC.

[Scene 27]

With my left eye pinned tight to my .50-caliber scope, I looked through the gap of the wooden window to where Catherine was being held and saw a struggle between her and the captor. The other bad guy was already on top of the other lady.

[Scene 28]

I focused my scope on the man who had just wrestled Catherine to the ground, took a deep breath, placed my finger on the trigger, and said the first two sentences in the Bull's prayer.

Me: "The lord is my shepherd. I shall not want."

[BANG~]

I put another round in the head of the bad guy on top of the other lady and kept shooting until the remaining two bad guys outside the house went down. Then I kept constant watch on the building through my scope as I ran towards the village.

[Scene 29]

The remaining captors had no idea what had just happened in the building where Catherine was being held. They were more interested in the dead villagers' valuables.

[Scene 30]

I entered the building from a rear window and secured Catherine. Both women were seated on the floor, shivering with fear.

Me: "Catherine Marlene, I'm Neil, United States Marines. I'm here to rescue you."

I carried both ladies in my arms to a dark corner of the room and covered them with a sack I found there.

I called Command and informed them that the hostage was secured. Then I positioned myself close to the door. A silent Beretta M9 was in my left hand, and a Gerber Mark 2 was gripped tight in my right palm. The feeling going through my body resembled the one you get when your supervisor tells you to leave everything you're doing and report to his office right away. My anxiety increased with every bit of sound around me. The hum of grieving villagers bustled in distance.

The sky was just giving way to the sun when I peeped through the slightly open door beside me. It was as if one of the bad guys had been standing there waiting for me to open the door. I charged toward him faster than he could react and stabbed him in the throat. One twist from the knife ended his life instantly. Five down, eight to go.

Just after I dragged the dead body inside the room, I heard someone speaking a foreign language approaching the building.

[Scene 31]

Soldier: "Yordani. Rosel. Donde demonios estas? Donde estan los dos rehenes?"

[Scene 32]

I understood and spoke a little Spanish, so I replied.

Me: "Dormido. Ellos estan durmiendo. Lo tengo

cubiertos. Gracias."

He'd asked what was going on with the hostages. Pretending to be one of the bad guys, I'd told him the hostages were sleeping. He seemed to sense something was wrong. His AK-47 was drawn as he carefully walked towards the door.

[Scene 33]

I whispered the Bull's prayer gently and put two rounds in his chest when he came close to the door.

Somehow, he managed to discharge a round before he fell. I put another round in his head as he was trying to stand up, and he went down permanently.

[Scene 34]

The sound from his AK-47 alerted the remaining bad guys, who were on the other side of the building. Seven of them ran towards the house, not knowing what to expect.

[Scene 35]

Just as I was preparing for a gunfight with seven

heavily armed men, I heard the distinctive sound of an Apache helicopter coming from the horizon.

[Scene 36]

I looked outside through the window and saw five American Apache helicopters approaching the village in all their exotic might and terrifying glory. I breathed a sigh of relief.

[Scene 37]

Instead of looking for a way to escape, the seven remaining bad guys turned their AK-47s to the Apaches and opened fire. It was a wrong decision that cost them their lives. All it took was a two-second round of fire from one Apache, and the seven of them were blown to pieces.

[Scene 38]

I was getting Catherine ready for the evacuation when I noticed I was slowly fainting away. I removed my armored vest and saw I'd been hit in the abdomen. I managed to carry her in my arm as I stumbled out waving an orange handheld smoke flare.

[Scene 39]

A Navy SEAL took my sniper's rifle and Beretta while another identified Catherine. I could hear the SEALs talking to Catherine as they rushed me to the helicopter on a stretcher. That was the last thing I remembered.

[Scene 40]

[Washington Hospital, Florida]

Rays of white fluorescent light radiated across the ceiling. Seconds after seconds, I listened to the hand of the clock ticking as I slowly opened my eyes at the military Washington Hospital in Langley, Florida. I whispered to the nurse standing on my left side.

Me: "Where is Catherine?"

Nurse: "Hey, you're awake."

I nodded yes while touching the stitches on my

abdomen with my right finger.

Me: "Where is Catherine?"

Nurse: "I'm not sure who Catherine is. Is that your girlfriend?"

I shook my head.

Nurse: "Okay. There's someone outside. I'll get him for you."

John Brown, a Marine first lieutenant stationed in Florida, and Dr. Chad entered the room.

Dr. Chad: "Hey, Neil, I'm Doctor Chad, Marine Corps medic. I'm one of the doctors who performed the surgery on you. How're you feeling?"

Me: "How long have I been here?"

Dr. Chad: "Two days. They brought you here on Saturday. I need you to get more rest. I'll leave you some prescriptions. Hope you get better soon. Here's Lieutenant Brown. He's the one assigned to watch you tonight. Take care, Neil. I'll see you tomorrow."

Doctor Chad exited the room.

Lieutenant Brown: "Captain, how're you feeling?"

Me: "Good."

Lieutenant Brown: "Good, good, I'm glad to hear that. I've heard about you. You're the first person to qualify for all special operations forces. I also heard you can sniff with the capacity of a German Shepherd. Much respect, bro. I've been in the Marine Corps for two years, and I didn't know such training existed in the military. Who trained you, bro?"

I mumbled the reply with my mouth barely open.

Me: "Nature."

There was a short silence before Lieutenant Brown responded.

Lieutenant Brown: "That could only be the right answer, man, 'cause I've never heard of anyone who could sniff like a dog. And in case you haven't heard, the news of the rescue mission was on the news this morning. The SEALs who were supposed to carry out the operation said you did it all by yourself. To be honest, bro, that was cold. That's some shit that only a SEAL or a Ranger could do.

"These nurses here are so freaking mean. None of them would wait three minutes and let me smoke outside. Except one. Her name is Chelsea. She only comes in at midnight, though. She's the only one who waited yesterday and let me smoke outside. She's cute, too; you're gonna like her. I promise, bro, you will fall in love with her at first sight."

On certain occasions, a soldier who is injured during a classified operation may be assigned a watcher during his recovery. The lieutenant assigned to watch me that night was one hell of a watcher. He was more likely to kill me with his mouth than the gunshot wound on my abdomen.

He said he hadn't heard of anyone who could sniff like a dog. I hadn't heard of any Marine lieutenant who talked that much either.

But he was right. I was twenty-eight that night

when I first met Chelsea, the assistant nurse he was talking about. I fell in love with her at first sight.

[Scene 41]

Five months after my recovery, Chelsea and I got married, and a year later, we had our first daughter. I named her after Catherine, the female hostage I was trying to rescue in Cuba when I got shot.

[Scene 42]

Chelsea was two months pregnant the day Catherine celebrated her tenth birthday. The following week, I would be starting my fourth year in college.

I'd just brought in a pack of caparison for the kids at the birthday party when I received a call from the Marine base in Houston, Texas. I was ordered to report to the nearest military base in Florida that night. Chelsea was standing beside me when I answered the phone call. Though the only words that came out of my mouth when I was on the phone were "Yes, sir," she didn't ask who had called or what we had talked about. The look on my face when I hung up said it all.

It wasn't the first time she saw that look on my face. Times without number, I'd left her in the middle of a vacation to report for military duty.

[Scene 43]

Chelsea went upstairs, while I headed to the basement to prepare my stuff.

I knew she was upset, but I had no choice. There're two calls in life you can't refuse: death, and military duty. We've had some minor disagreements in our relationship, and we fixed them. Trust is the only thing that can't be fully restored when it's broken. I haven't crossed that line yet.

My mother once told me the only time she'd ever seen me cry was at the hospital when she'd given birth to me. I didn't know how that could be possible, but I never doubted it. As far back as I can think, I don't remember a time when tears rolled down my cheeks. My mind somehow found a way to conceal my feelings.

[Scene 44]

Catherine would have been upset if she'd known I was leaving the party, so I snuck out quietly through the door in the basement.

Cataphrase B

"Wise people know that time means money.
That's why they spend a lot of money advertising
on social networks: because they know stupid
people spend all their time there."

— Teni A.

[Scene 45]

The nearest military base from my house was Olney base in Miami. I got there before sundown.

A little over five thousand troops were already at the base. America wasn't involved in any apparent war; hence, I didn't know if the preparation was a drill or for another classified operation. No one could tell. It didn't matter to us anyway. We were ready to go to the end of the world as soon as they gave us the order.

At 9am the following morning, the first briefing would commence. By then, everyone on base would have completed a seven-mile run and at least two hundred push-ups.

The suspicion among the troops that night was that we were going after a terrorist leader who had eluded the CIA for years.

[Scene 46]

[9am, August 5, 2007]

Just as everyone had suspected, the mission was to kill or capture Asheem, a terrorist leader hiding in Lebanon.

Two Army platoons and a battalion would assault Salaban, a town in Lebanon where Asheem Ralab was hiding. My unit would join the mission to provide sniper cover as the troops carried out the operation. The Lebanon mission was code named "Iron."

Between Green Apple and Iron, I had done operation Rainbow, ASCAP, Romeo, and, the most famous of all, Miracle.

During operation Miracle, I eliminated eighty-seven combatants with a knife and my bare hands. Miracle earned me the respect of every Marine in the nation.

When the aftermath footage of Miracle was played on the news, no one could believe that one human alone had inflicted such devastation. Thus, contrary to what the evidence revealed, the government of Chad, where the mission had taken place, concluded that the dead terrorists had been attacked by wild beasts.

When I returned home from Operation Miracle, the top military officials who knew I'd carried out the mission alone dubbed me "the Beast." I was known among the rest of the military as "the Green Viper."

****

[Scene 47]

Forty-five camps on the base sheltered all the troops. I'd just completed my seven-mile run when, somehow, I walked into the wrong camp as I was looking for mine.

[Scene 48]

[Inside Platoon 8's camp]

Soldier: "Look who we got here, fellas. The devil doesn't need an introduction. It's the one and only Green Viper. I'm Moses Phillip, Platoon 8, United States Army."

Me: "Nice to meet you, Moses. I'm Captain Bull, Marine Corps."

Moses: "Like I said, the devil doesn't need an introduction."

Me: "Is this your first deployment?"

Moses: "You can tell Baby, I can't wait to start kicking ass."

Me: "Have you been in a combat situation before?"

Moses: "No, but I'm not afraid, if that's what you're thinking. *This is Platoon 8, baby.* We're the best. Hey, I promise, man, if I have Asheem in my sight, I won't miss the shot."

Me: "I'll remember you said so. Do you know any fast way I can take to the Marine camp?"

Moses: "There's no fast way around here, bro. There's only one way to heaven, same way you came."

Me: "I get it. Nice talking to you, Moses."

Moses: "Nice talking to you, too."

[Scene 49]

Marine officers are very disciplined, but sometimes, they can act like assholes when playing around.

A group of Marines were pulling Paul's leg— he had a stammer—when I walked inside the camp.

One of the Marine officers, Bob Martins, was asking, "What's the name of the longest river in America?"

Marine Officer: "Ask Paul. He's good at geography."

Bob: "Hey, Paul, do you remember the name of the longest river in America? It just escaped my mind."

Paul: "Mi-Mi-Mi-Mi-ssissippi."

Bob: "Is that a new state *in* America?"

Marine **Officer:** "Yeah, that's the state where Paul attended high school. Mi-Mi-Mi-Mi-ssissippi. You haven't heard about it, Bob?"

Bob: "I have. Isn't that where the Vikings discovered the Garden of Eden?"

Marine **Officer:** "*You got it*. The Holy Land where Paul and Charles Darwin discovered the Neanderthals. The Mi-Mi-Mi-Mi-ssissipi."

Paul: "Fuck you."

Everyone laughed.

Me: "Enough!"

Bob: "Woo . . . Look who's here, the legendary Green Viper. Today must be Halloween."

Everyone laughed.

Me: "Yeah, today is the devil's birthday. And whose birthday are we celebrating tomorrow in Lebanon?"

Bob: "Paul's."

Everyone responded with a little laugh.

Me: "No, I think it's you, Bob. Your assignment for tomorrow has changed. You will be joining Charley Team to provide backup for Platoon 8."

Marine **O**fficer: "BAM!"

Marine Officer: "Damn, Bob, you are babysitting

the platoon rookies tomorrow? That sucks."

Bob (to me): "You're kidding me, right?"

Me: "No, I'm not."

Bob: "That wasn't my initial assignment for tomorrow. I was assigned as your spotter."

Me: "*Welcome to the Marines*, bro."

Bob: "Hold on, I'm going to check that with the colonel."

Bob walked out of the camp.

Me: "Alright guys, Bob's assignment didn't change. I just wanted him to take the dumb walk for disrespecting Paul. Guys, all of us are grown men. Let's show each other some respect."

Marine Officer: "Oh . . shit. He's going to be mad as hell when he comes back."

Me: "That's fine. What goes around comes around."

I'd been on a mission before in Lebanon and many

other countries. Some of those Marine officers hadn't been outside America, let alone been on a mission. Most especially, Bob had joined the mission two months after his Marine Corps graduation. He was considered the best in his regiment.

[Scene 50]

[Lebanon]

We left Miami the following day around 5 pm and arrived in Lebanon some few minutes before midnight. No defense radar spotted our plane. We entered the country as if we were invited for a dinner party.

Two roads led to Salaban. Two platoons, a thousand each, would invade from both entrances until they were joined by another battalion, and then they would zero in on the target. A little over ten snipers, including myself, were positioned half a mile around the target building.

[Scene 51]

Early that morning, the operation began. Bob and I spent few minutes camouflaging our sniping post while getting to know each other.

As Bob was lying down, adjusting his binoculars, he said something I suspected he was going to say.

Bob: "It's an honor being on a mission with you, Viper."

He said it like I was some kind of super viper-man going around biting people.

Me: "We are all heroes. Bob, there's one rule I give to every spotter who calls my shots during a combat situation."

Bob: "What is it?"

Me: "Don't tell me to shoot a human you don't intend to kill."

Bob (with a smile): "Don't tell a Marine officer to shoot a human you don't intend to kill."

Some seconds passed.

Me: "Quick question, Bob. When you wipe your ass, do you look at the tissue paper with your eyes or your brain?"

Bob: "I look at the tissue with my eyes. You?"

Me: "Nope. Only fools look at the tissue with their eyes when they wipe their ass. Reasonably speaking, your brain should tell you that the first wipe would be dirty; thus, you don't have to look at the first wipe. If you keep wiping until your anus is no longer slippery, your brain should tell you that your ass is clean. That's how blind people wipe their ass."

Bob: "So . . . what's the logic, Neil? A guy like you won't ask such questions without a reason."

Me: "Some years ago, when the CIA first attempted to capture or kill Asheem, I was the sniper on the mission."

Bob: "You've been here before?"

Me: "Yeah, before you joined the Marine Corps. My spotter, a high school friend, was lying next to me, like you are doing right now, when a sniper round penetrated his scope and killed him instantly. That bullet was meant for me, but I was lucky.

"Alone in the mountains, with just the scope on

my rifle, I used my brain as my spotter and took out the sniper who killed Math, a mile and a half away."

Bob: "I've heard of the mile-and-a-half kill. I didn't know it happened without a spotter."

Me: "So, God forbid, Bob, but just in case I'm not so lucky this time, I'm gonna need you to take these shots by yourself. And in case you think it can't be done, think of how blind people look at the tissue when they wipe their ass."

Bob: "Nothing bad will happen to you. I'm sorry about your friend."

[Scene 52]

As soon as the cover of darkness cleared, everything that could go wrong went wrong in Salaban.

[Scene 53]

Through my scope, I saw one of our Humvees on fire. Bob called in a position. When I looked there, four enemies were positioning a mortar. He gave me my coordinates. Wind direction, distance, and other adjustments. I took a deep breath, placed my finger on the trigger, and said the Bull's prayer.

Bob: "FIRE!"

[BANG~]

I fired a shot at the enemy's mortar shell, and five of them went down.

Bob: "Enemies down. Another one to the left—two of them by the white van."

Me: "I got 'em."

Before I could take the shot, the two enemies behind the white van went down. Another Marine sniper in the area must have taken the shot.

[Scene 54]

Across from the main target, about ten yards away, there was an abandoned building standing alone. Groups of our soldiers were making their way out of the damaged building towards the targeted house when a couple of them started falling.

[Scene 55]

Instinctively, I knew there was an enemy sniper somewhere taking out our soldiers.

[Scene 56]

The remaining soldiers immediately retreated and took cover behind the damaged building.

[Scene 57]

All Marine snipers in the area shifted their attention to every rooftop in the area, scouting for anything suspicious.

For about half an hour, all the Marine snipers, including me and Bob, scanned the area, but to no avail.

[Scene 58]

One soldier behind the abandon building attempted to run for it, but a bullet struck his helmet and killed him. One invincible sniper had brought the whole operation to a standstill.

[Scene 59]

We weren't going to sit there forever, not when I knew exactly what to do. I'd been on a mission there before. The only way to find a sniper around there was to go out and look for him or her.

I handed my sniper rifle to Bob and told him something he would later understand when he saw it.

Me: "Follow the old lady."

I grabbed a small bag from my backpack and ran towards the exit door.

Bob: "What old lady? Hold on, man. Where're you going? Wait, I'm following you."

Me: "No." I stopped and turned to Bob. "Don't follow me. Follow the old lady."

Bob: "What old lady are you talking about, man? You're the only one here with me. *I don't see no old lady.*"

Me: "That's because you're still looking at the tissue with your eyes. Bob, look at the tissue with your brain. Get back on your scope and follow the old lady."

[Scene 60]

Bob stood still with my rifle in his hand, looking at me with confusion as I ran towards the exit door.

I left the room in a complete Marine uniform, but when I emerged from the front door downstairs and moved approximately three blocks away from the building, what Bob saw through his scope was a steadily walking old lady in a hijab. I blended in with the locals and made my way into the town.

[Scene 61]

Bob (over the radio): "Viper, is that you? *Yo*, what the hell are you doing, man?"

Me: "Follow the old lady."

Bob: "Damn it, I knew that was you. Where the hell did you get that dress?"

Me: "I don't know. It doesn't matter. Just follow the old lady."

Bob: "Roger that, Viper. I'm on you."

Just like a jet stream trails a jet, when a sniper shoots a target, he or she leaves a trail of his own location behind. The reason is because bullets only travel in a straight line. And unless the laws of nature have changed, for every action, there's an equal and opposite reaction.

If you can't get close to a sniper's victim to start your trail towards the sniper, follow a forty-five-degree angle in the opposite direction of the entry wound. That path will lead you in the direction the shot was fired from.

The second approach is to assume that a sniper will stay within the max range of his or her gun. Since every round has a maximum range, the distance between a sniper and his target could, in most cases, be measured by the force of impact, the density of the target, and the type of round used.

When the target is a human wearing no protective clothing, if the bullet penetrated and lodged in the target, the sniper should be approximately ¾ of the max range of the round used or more. If the bullet entered and exited the victim's body, the sniper is approximately half the max range of the round used or less.

A sniper who has fired numerous shots on different targets with different guns from different distances and has thoroughly examined how the bullets penetrated the targets should be able to predict the distance of a sniper if he or she examines the victim.

During my sniper training, I fired over nine thousand shots with different guns and ammunitions and at different targets ranging from armored vests to armored cars, concrete walls, rocks, ballistic-gelatin backed and not-backed armored vests, and thoroughly examined all of them. Because of this, I can determine the enemy sniper's position if someone describes to me the wound of one of the dead soldiers.

[Scene 62]

After I walked about seven yards away from Bob's position, in the direction where I believed the shots were fired from, I stopped and radioed the soldiers that were pinned behind the enemy line.

[Radio conversation]

Me: "Platoon 8, this is Charley Freedom. Do you copy?"

Someone from Platoon 8: "Yes, I do. Charley Freedom, we are in serious trouble. We're pinned down by a sniper. Four of my men are down. I repeat, four soldiers are dead."

Me: "Copy that, Platoon 8. We're aware of your situation. Platoon 8, I need you to do something for me. If you can get hold of one of your dead soldiers, can you remove his vest and describe the gunshot wound, starting from the point of impact. And if possible, I need a description of the bullet that killed the soldier."

Someone from Platoon 8: "What! Describing the wound won't save their lives; I told you they are dead. We need help."

Me: "Moses, is that you? This voice sounds familiar."

Moses: "Yeah, who's this?"

Me: "This is Green viper."

[Scene 63]

Moses: "Holy shit. Hey, guys, I got Green Viper on line. Hey, man, we're in serious trouble. Where are you?"

[Scene 64]

Me: "I can't tell you where I am, Moses, but I can guarantee you that if you describe that wound to me, you will be out of there soon. I know describing the wound won't resurrect your dead soldiers, but it could save your life and the rest of your platoon. So, soldier, are you gonna give me what I asked for?"

Moses: "Yes, sir. Give me a second . . . One shot, center mass. The bullet penetrated his armored vest and entered the chest through the top left lung. One exit wound on the body. The bullet punched the rear vest, but didn't exit the rear part of the vest. The bullet is a .264 caliber, 6.7 mm. Do you copy?"

Me: "Yeah, I copy. Thanks, Moses. You are a hero."

The max range of a .264 caliber bullet is about nine hundred yards. But with the description of the wound inflicted by the 6.7mm round, I predicted the enemy sniper position to be approximately 0.3 miles away (three hundred yards). That was less than what I'd originally thought.

[Scene 65]

With the information I'd received from Moses, I tracked the sniper's position to a building seven stories high, about 450 yards from my starting point. By then, I knew Bob would have lost track of the old lady. I stopped in a less crowded area and sat next to a mobile canteen like an old lady relaxing her legs after a long walk. Quietly, where I sat, I radioed Bob.

Me: "Bob, you still there?"

*****

Bob: "Yep, still following the old lady."

Me: "Good. Put your scope on the tall building to my right, the one with the Lebanese flag. Tell me what you see."

Bob: "Uh. . . nothing much is happening there. I see a couple of locals, women, kids, nothing strange."

Me: "Roger that. Look at the building on my left and observe the little damaged window by the chimney. Tell me what you see."

Bob: "Ten-four. *Damaged window on the left.* I can't see anything inside. It's too dark."

Me: "Keep your eyes on that window."

I radioed Platoon 8.

Me: "Charley Freedom to Platoon 8. Platoon 8, do you copy?"

[Scene 66]

[Behind enemy line]

Moses (over the radio): "Platoon 8, I copy. Where have you been?"

[Scene 67]

Me: "Moses, there's one more thing I need you to do for me. I need to smoke out this moron from wherever he's located, and you are the only one who can help me."

Moses: "Okay, what do you need me to do?"

Me: "The dead soldier you removed the vest from earlier, I need you to put his vest back on him and attach a gun to his hands."

Moses: "Okay."

Me: "Lay him straight up on the floor, chest face down. When you're done, I need you to get behind his foot. Hold him by his shoes and gently push him out of concealment. By doing so, you will create to the enemy sniper an impression that one of you is trying to sneak out of the sniper's line of fire."

[Scene 68]

Moses: "Roger that, Charley, I'm on it."

[Scene 69]

[Two minutes later]

Bob (over the radio): "Shot fired, shot fired. Viper, I saw a muzzle flash at the damaged window."

[Scene 70]

Moses (over the radio): "Shot fired, Charley Freedom. Enemy sniper just fired at the dead soldier."

[Scene 71]

Me (over the radio): "Roger that, Moses."

Me (to myself): "I got you, son of a bitch."

Me (over the radio): "Bob, take the shot when you're ready."

[Scene 72]

Bob: "Roger that, Charley. I can't see where the sniper is positioned in the room. It's too dark."

Me: "You don't have to, Bob. Look at the window

with your brain. Your distance from the target is approximately 450 yards. Fire when you're ready. If you miss, I'll take care of the target down here."

Bob: "Copy."

[Scene 73]

Some seconds later, Bob fired a shot and hit the enemy sniper in the arm.

[Scene 74]

Bob: "Charley, sniper is hit but still moving. He has exited the room."

[Scene 75]

Me: "Roger that, I'm on him."

My silent Beretta M9 was pointed out as I entered the first floor of the building. A gunfight broke out the moment I shot the first combatant watching the entrance. One after another, I took out three enemies watching the first-floor entrance.

I proceeded to the second floor with my gun still drawn. A hunting upsurge of silence followed me as I made my way upstairs.

[Scene 76]

On the sixth floor, I could tell someone was in one of the rooms. Every sound I heard sent me moving more quickly, yet I maintained complete silence when I was clearing each closet in the room.

There were two damaged brown doors blocking the entrance of the last room on the floor.

[Scene 77]

I glanced between the gaps of the damaged door and saw the enemy sniper administering first aid to the wound on his arm. His rifle sat on the floor as I approached him cautiously from behind. I pressed my silent Beretta to the back of his head when I got behind him. He didn't look back when he spoke to me.

Sniper: "Who are you?"

[Silence]

Sniper: "What do you want?"

Me: "The lord is my shepherd. I shall not want."

[BANG~]

I fired a shot to the back of his head, and he went down for good. One shot, one kill. The last thing he heard was the Bull's prayer. I hope it rang in his ears as he rode the wild bull to hell.

[Radio conversation]

Me: "Platoon 8, this is Charley Freedom. You are cleared to proceed with your mission. Enemy sniper is down. I repeat, enemy sniper is down."

Moses: "Copy that, Charley Freedom."

****

[Scene 78]

The raid continued into the afternoon. With the sun blazing like a furnace, Platoon 8 and the 4th Battalion carried out the mission successfully.

The death of Asheem brought a huge relief to the Israeli government, who had been at war for two years with Sahian, an extremist group created by Asheem when he'd been alive.

I was fourteen when my father died. My mother had to work two jobs to take care of me and my two sisters. Despite all the circumstances I faced when I was growing up, I never allowed my challenges in life to stop me from achieving my goals. I did what every man was expected to do: I went to college, got married, raised three kids, and, above all, served my country with respect and dignity.

[Scene 79]

After serving twenty-three years in the Marine Corps, on June 3, 2017, I was appointed as the commandant general of the Marine Corps.

I don't know who said lightning never strikes the same place twice. But on June 3, it happened at the Pentagon. The same day I was made a marine general, the assistant commandant of the Marine Corps was also appointed. It was nobody else other than my old Marine spotter, Bob Martins. The last time we'd seen each other had been in Lebanon, after I'd eliminated the enemy sniper.

I'd heard of Bob's excellence and accomplishments in the Marine Corps. It was amazing how, after so many years, we had been appointed to work together again. Bob often reminded me of Mathew, my high school friend who had been killed during a classified operation in Lebanon.

Every Veteran's Day, regardless of weather conditions, I'm always at Arlington Cemetery, at Math's grave, paying my respect.

Cataphrase C

"I can tolerate the annoying buzz of a mosquito in my ears. What I can't stand is the voice of a healthy man complaining about hard work."

—Teni A.

[Scene 80]

[Arlington Cemetery]

The afternoon sky was shucking down heavy rain at the Arlington cemetery. It was the first Veterans Day after I became Marine General, and as usual, I was at Math's grave paying my respect.

As the rain shower was washing me like laundry, a familiar voice behind me recited my old Marine poem.

Voice: *"Once a Marine . . . always a Marine.*
The shield around me isn't hard or soft. It's just a shield from my own imagination. I'm always courageous as if the shield is real.

What has a man who lost his fear in battle had to fear? Even when I'm faced with fire, I'm as brave as water. Gentle in my talk, but loud in my actions. I do to others as I would do to myself.

When others asked for peace, they gave me a rifle. When everyone asked for riches, I just want the simple things in life: love, liberty, and happiness. *Maybe a little nice old country Cadillac if life is so kind.* If not, I'll accept the rodeo and move on. My approach to life is simple: live it or leave it. And until the day my strength fades away, the day the lion can no longer hunt, the day my eyelids close and my gray hair falls out, I'll continue to fight the fight of freedom and sing the song of hope. Because *once a Marine . . . always a Marine.*"

That was Bob reciting my Marine poem. He covered me with an umbrella as we walked back to the car.

[Scene 81]

We planned to take the local road back to the Pentagon, but due to traffic, we headed towards the toll road.

Bob and I were discussing if I should stop at the nearest hotel to change my wet uniform when his phone rang.

Bob (on the phone): "Hello. Yes, sir. . . Yes, sir. He's here with me. Sure. I'll let him know right away."

Me: "Who was that?"

Bob: "The president has been trying to reach you.

Where is your phone?"

Me: "In the glove box, damn it. I left it in the car because of the rain."

I brought out my cell phone from the glove box.

Me: "Damn! Seven missed calls. What did he say?"

Bob: "He wants you to call him right away."

I telephoned the president.

Me: "Mr. President, this is General Bull speaking."

President: "General, I need you to report to the Oval Office right away."

Me: "I'm on my way, sir. ETA is forty minutes."

[Scene 82]

The majority of the Joint Chiefs of Staff were seated in the Oval Office when I arrived there. The Navy commandant asked where I'd been, as if he didn't know that it was Veterans Day. The news was about Bahad, the brother of Asheem.

Navy Commandant (to me): "The FBI raided the apartment of Bahad Asheem in Texas early this morning. General, what they found inside the apartment was what we already suspected."

Me: "Let me guess, explosives."

Navy Commandant: "Yep. He was heading towards a Marine barrack in El Paso with a car full of TNT when he was arrested by the FBI this morning.

"According to a diary found in his apartment, his other targets included every military barrack in the United States, a train station in Chicago, the White House, and a shopping mall in Texas. The FBI told us you know Asheem's family more than any intelligence agency in America. General, are there any other family members connected to Asheem inside or outside the United States that we need to know of?"

Me: "Bahad is the only family member I know of inside the United States. I believe the rest of them live outside the country. I advised the FBI to keep an eye on Bahad the moment he arrived in Texas some years ago."

Navy Commandant: "I'm glad you did. Otherwise, by now, you'd be preparing to clean up the pieces of a bunch of Marine officers. However, the president believes this threat is a matter of national security. Every military base in the country has been put on high alert. That also includes the Marine base in Washington where you live.

"This extra measure will be fully enforced until we can assure the president that the treat has been completely eliminated."

Me: "If the president wants full assurance, he knows exactly what to do. This isn't the first time we've faced retaliation from a late terrorist's relative. What will it cost the president to pen a law that will stop this type of incident from happening again?"

Navy Commandant: "I've asked myself that question a thousand times, but General, my job is to command the Navy and give military advice to the president. I don't make laws."

[Scene 83]

I wish the president had been there that evening. I would have asked him the question directly. That is one thing the president and I have in common: we can't hide our feelings. When I speak, I speak freely and openly. God hasn't created a human I can't speak to.

Every year, the United States government gives millions of dollars to help other countries eliminate poverty. Yet in our own country, there're homeless kids who don't have a place to sleep.

The United States government has donated billions of dollars towards health care in other countries, yet in America, there are millions of people who can't afford health care.

It is only after evil has happened to us that we remember to make drastic changes.

We've opened records on our citizens that only have space for wrongdoings. If I spank a child, for instance, they will add the incident to my record. What about when I risked my life to save a child from a burning building? Don't I deserve a record for the good things I've done, just as I do for the mistakes I've made?

I'm not saying all problems that appear less complicated are easy to solve. Most of the problems facing a well-developed country contain more complexities than apparent simplicities. However, the solutions to some of these problems are like adult movies. You don't have to be a superstar to act in a porn movie.

When I joined the Marine Corps, I pledged to serve America and defend her liberty. But I knew I couldn't solve America's problem if I were still taking orders from a leader who was not willing to solve the problem. I'm just prey if I'm inside a tiger's cage trying to feed the beast. I must find a way to get outside the cage if I want to succeed.

What I said I would have told the president the other day if he were in the Oval Office was what I told him the next day when we met at the Senate Building.

George Frankfort (the US president then) was one hell of a human being. The reply he gave me was what I suspected he was going to say. He said, "General, it's not too late to run for office. When you become president, you can sign whatever bill you want into law."

And that's exactly what I did. After I served a

few months as marine general, I ran for the highest office in the nation, and I won.

[Scene 84]

[Back to January 20 (Scene 1) Inauguration Day.]

Chief Justice: "I first met Mr. Bull a year ago when he was still the Marine Commandant. His voice was what captured my attention. He stood in the middle of a hallway at the Supreme Court Building here in Washington, speaking to a lady beside me like he was commanding a thousand troops.

"I introduced myself to him that day, and since then, we have become friends. Today, I'm glad to introduce him to you once again, a man who walks with swagger and majesty. Ladies and gentlemen, it is my honor to present the president of the United States of America, Neil Kenneth Bull."

[A continuous round of applause from the audience]

Me: "Thank you. Chief Justice, President Frankfort, distinguished ladies and gentlemen, thank you.

"Today marks the forty-seventh time we've carried on a legacy that started almost two hundred years ago.

"America became independent in the year 1776. Since then, on the twentieth of January, every four years, people gather together on this hill to inaugurate a president, a citizen chosen by the people, with the hope that he will deliver the change and better life they deserve. If he fails, they either gave him another chance, as the Constitution allows, or they elect another citizen.

"Before me, many Americans took the oath of office. Some finished their terms, some were impeached, and some died during their time in office.

"As usual, we've gathered together once again, and from the candidates who ran for the presidency this election, you chose me to be your next president. I will forever be grateful for the honor and trust you have in me."

[Audience applause]

Me: "I was once a Marine, and in my mind, I'll always be a Marine. I believe actions speak louder than words. So, today, my speech will be short, but clear and precise.

"America's greatest resource isn't her economy or our technologies. Neither is it the power retained in our military. America's greatest resource is its citizens.

"Therefore, from today, and until the day I'm no longer president of the United States of America, the first, most important priority of the United States government at home and abroad is its citizens."

[A continuous round of applause from the audience]

Me: "We learn from history that a country thrives when the citizens are doing well and a person does well if he can put food on the table and take care of his family. Yet the greatest wealth of a human isn't the things he can afford, nor is it the treasure that he has stored. A human's greatest wealth is his health. That leads me to my next agenda, health care.

"My fellow Americans, the era of waiting is over. The days of our groaning has come to end today. An average middle-class person spends his or her tax return on temporary things in less than a month. That money can be used to fight a problem that has taken more American lives than every enemy America has ever known.

"So, my first week in office, I'll work with Congress to create a plan that will allow working Americans to choose between getting back their federal tax return or putting it towards getting health care coverage. When you select the option to put your federal tax return towards getting health care coverage, any amount left over after a thousand dollars will be returned to you when you file your taxes. And as I mentioned during my campaign, this plan only applies to federal taxes, not state taxes. I'll also include in the bill free health care for every American soldier who is injured in battle."

[A continuous round of applause from the audience]

Me: "Now, that's just common sense. If you send a healthy man to war and he returns with a limb missing, you should at least do something to take care of him."

[A continuous round of applause from the audience]

Me: "I'll work with scientists and governments here at home and around the world to combat climate change, fight diseases, and bring an end to poverty.

"I'll propose education reform that will make college affordable, and if Congress can reach a bilateral agreement, a free community college education will start very soon in America."

[A continuous round of applause by the audience]

Me: "To those who embrace the path of freedom and equality, those who deter tyranny and segregation and condemn terrorism, I want you to know America is your friend, and my administration will work with you every step of the way to maintain and restore prosperity and strengthen human rights.

"To those who choose the path of evil over peace, those who threaten our ways of life and spread the message of terror and fear, your days are numbered.

"I didn't run for the presidency to start a war with terrorism, but during my time in office, if any terrorist dares to touch any one of these people, whether here in America or outside America, I promise I'll find you, I'll expose you, and I'll show you the merciless face of America's military might. I've dealt with you before when I was a soldier taking orders, and I'm more determined to deal with you now that I'm the commander in chief of the armed forces.

"Not everyone knows it, but every human has his own rules. Mine is simple: don't piss me off. I can be your sweetest dream or your worst nightmare. You get to choose.

"To every nation watching around the world, I want you to know America is your friend. It's been our nation's core principle to promote peace and liberty, strengthen the weak, and give a helping hand to those who are willing to enforce human rights, and as America's next president, I'm ready to work with you to make this world a better place. Thank you. Thank you, everyone."

I turned away from the microphone after the speech and said the Bull's prayer silently while waving my hand to greet the audience.

[Scene 85]

At the Capitol Building that day, just like a new hire

would do, I signed a bunch of papers. Unlike your usual new employee at Chipotle, I was assigned power over all United States nuclear weapons.

[Scene 86]

On Inauguration Day, before I went to bed, I, the first lady, and the kids had our first dinner at the White House.

[At the dining table in the White house]

Me: "Guys, how is the food?"

Mariah (my younger daughter): "Good, did the Secret Service cook this pasta, Dad?"

Me: "Why?"

Mariah: "It tastes so good—I'm convinced there's a secret ingredient in it."

Catherine: "Whatever. It's just an ordinary pasta cooked with olive oil and tomato paste, nothing special."

Mariah: "Yeah, right. 'Ordinary pasta cooked with olive oil and tomato paste.' Like you've had some before."

Catherine: "Yeah, I have."

Mariah: "Cooked in the White House?"

Catherine: "No. Does it matter where food is cooked? I've been to a nice Italian restaurant before, *White House girl!*"

Michael (my youngest child): "Ha, ha, both of you are now White House girls."

Chelsea: "That's enough, guys. Some chefs you will get to know later cooked the pasta. There's nothing special about it."

A Secret Service agent, Jeff, entered the dining room.

Jeff: "Mr. President, the Beast is ready in case you still want to visit the vice president's place tonight."

Michael: "Woo! *The Beast,' 'Mr. President.'* Dad, or Mr. President, whichever one you prefer, can we finish our dinner before you and the *'Beast'* take another trip together again tonight, please?"

Me: "I'm not going anywhere tonight, guys. Jeff, please call the vice president and tell him I'll see him tomorrow. I need to get some rest."

Jeff: "No problem, sir. I'll let him know."

[Scene 87]

Later that night, Chelsea and I chatted on the bed before we slept.

Chelsea: "Nice bed."

Me: "Really."

Chelsea: "I'm just saying it feels a little better than that old king-size mattress we slept on for five years."

Me: "Now you sound like Mariah earlier at the dinner table."

Chelsea: "She was right. Seriously, that pasta tasted so delicious—I'm also convinced there's a secret ingredient in it."

Me: "Okay, it's time to sleep. It seems as if you and the kids have had too much stress today, because I didn't notice anything special about that pasta or this bed."

Chelsea: "Maybe not the pasta, but this bed is great. You know I can tell if a bed is good after we make love on it. Like the one at the hotel room where we stayed during our vacation last year in Japan. Do you remember?"

Me: "I don't remember. Speaking of Japan, it's possible that could be my first foreign visit."

Chelsea: "You mean that could be 'OUR' first foreign visit?"

Me: "Honey, there's only one president here."

Chelsea: "No, there're two presidents here. Wherever you go, the kids and I are coming with you."

Me: "They resume school very soon. They won't

have time for trips."

Chelsea: *"I do."*

[Scene 88]

A week after we moved into the White house, Catherine resumed school at the college in Florida she attended while Mariah and Michael started their new school there in Washington, DC. The same week, I started preparing my first bill.

I'd promised during my campaign that within my first hundred days, I would work on national security and health care. The health care reform bill had been a little hard to push through Congress. However, my first two months in office, I was able to accomplish national security reform.

[Scene 89]

On the 9th of April, three months after I became president, in front of all Americans, I signed the 707 bill into law. A lot of Americans found a huge relief in the reform bill, knowing they wouldn't have to worry about terrorists' relatives coming into the United States for retaliation.

However, not everyone was happy with the bill. I wasn't surprised, since not every bill signed into law by the president is satisfactory to the people.

Most people argued that in the future, the bill might open the door for hard immigration rules on foreigners. I'm sure the same kind of people said the same thing about the second amendment.

If that's the case, I can also create a similar argument about an armored vehicle made to protect the passengers, but that turns out to be a hard-to-escape box in an accident situation. Or a toilet designed to flush via motion sensor that keeps flushing the moment you sit on it.

The 707 bill would keep Americans safe at home from retaliatory attack. That was all that mattered to me. The following week, I attended my first Correspondents' Dinner.

[Scene 90]

[Correspondents' Dinner]

Me: "Thank you. I'm happy to be here today. I would have been happier if this was a correspondents' breakfast. This is the only correspondents" dinner where there's no dinner."

[Laughter]

Me: "All right, I see some familiar faces present here tonight. Kevin—is that you? You've changed. I have to thank Kevin especially for coming to the Correspondents' Dinner. The world wouldn't be exciting without short people. First, it was Gary Coleman; now it's you."

[Laughter]

Me: "For those who are wondering why I arrived late to the correspondents' Dinner this evening. I had to straighten up some things with my Secret Service agents before leaving the White House. For the agents that are not there this evening, I'm going to say it again one more time. Next time the first lady collapses, do not attempt a mouth-to-mouth resuscitation; that's the job of the president."

[Laughter]

Me: "I should make that the Twenty-eighth Amendment. Damn! The guy was all over my wife's mouth when I entered the room. I said, '*Guys, what the hell* is going on here?' The agent replied, 'Sir, we are trying to resuscitate the first lady." I said, 'Dawg! Resuscitate my ass.'"

[Laughter]

Me: "I have to thank the vice president for the great job he has been doing since we took office. I must confess, I'm proud of his noble commitment."

[A round of applause from the audience]

Me: "He is such a wonderful vice president. I mean, he's nice, he gets to work on time, he never misses an appointment, and he's never late to the Correspondents' Dinner; but sometimes he's a lot faster than expected.

"I had a dream recently that Air Force One got hijacked while the vice president and I were traveling together with some foreign delegates. When the Secret Service entered my room to rescue me, we looked around for the vice president and couldn't find him. So, I told the Secret Service agents to take me to the escape room. When we got there, we noticed the escape parachute had been deployed. The vice president had gotten there before me. He had escaped in my parachute."

[Laughter]

Me: "A few minutes later, I turned on the news, and he was already in Washington giving a speech."

[Laughter]

Me: "It turns out that the hijacking wasn't real. It was a drill. The Secret Service agents were just training.

"So, here I am, trying to explain to my foreign delegates why the vice president left Air Force One in an emergency pod that was design for the president.

"If you think that was all, wait until you hear what we saw next. We looked through Air force One's window and saw the Secretary of State dangling in a parachute."

[Laughter]

Me: "Unfortunately for her, when she jumped out of the plane, we were flying over Iranian territory."

[Laughter]

Me: "Now, that's a wrong place to land if you happen to be the United States Secretary of State."

[Laughter]

Me: "It was just a drill, for God's sake. What is wrong with these guys? Even the first lady failed the test."

[Laughter]

Me: "She was negotiating with the Secret Service agent who was acting like a terrorist when I arrived at the cockpit."

[Laughter]

Me: "She was about to give up her Facebook password when I told her the whole thing was a drill."

[Laughter]

Me: "She nearly punched the Secret Service agent

in the face when the guy told me her MySpace password is 32Karat underscore milkshake."

[Laughter]

Me: "She's a nice first lady."

[Applause]

Me: "It's just that things have changed since we started living in the White House. Sometimes, she has to leave the White House early, so often, I don't eat breakfast before leaving the house. That's why I wished earlier that this was a correspondents' breakfast."

[Laughter]

Me: "When I started losing weight as a result of malnutrition, everybody thought it was the first lady's healthy initiative plan that was working for me."

[Laughter]

Me: "Yeah, right. . . On Inauguration Day, after my

speech, a Secret Service agent came to me and said, 'Mr. President, the Beast is ready. When you're done, you can come and have a look.' The first lady replied, 'Who brought a beast to the Capitol Building? Tell them to return it to the zoo. I'm not comfortable around wild animals.'"

[Laughter]

Me: "I whispered gently into her ear, 'Honey, the Beast is not an animal; it's the president's armored limo.'"

[Laughter]

Me: The first lady is amazing. She went to China recently and came back with a reddish Chinese cheongsam dress that the first lady of China gave her as a present. When she got back to America, she put on the dress and said, 'Honey, I'm going to walk around the White House in this dress.' I said, 'No, no, no, honey, don't do it. There are snipers on the roof. They might confuse you with the White House crashers.'"

[Laughter]

Me: "I love the White House; it's one of the best houses in the world. My second day in the White House, I was highly disappointed because there were a lot of things I thought would be there, but they weren't. I guess I've been watching too many movies."

[Laughter]

Me: "So, I decided I was going to allow the tourists to find out the truth about the White House the same way I did.

"Last weekend, a group of tourists came to visit the White House. One of them stepped forward and asked, 'Mr. President, where is the blast-proof underground fish tank?' I replied, 'Go look for it in the basement.'

"After five minutes, they returned and said, 'Mr. President, we looked all over for the fish tank. We couldn't find it.' I said, 'Me either.'"

[Laughter]

Me: "They scratched their heads and remembered some other things they'd seen in the movies and said, 'Okay, Mr. President, where is the indestructible space shuttle built to carry the first family to space in case of a nuclear attack?' I replied, 'Oh! Go look for that one in the laundry room.'

"They went to the laundry room, and after five minutes of searching, they came back and said, 'Mr. President, we couldn't find the shuttle.' I said, 'Me either.'"

[Laughter]

Me: "One of the tourists decided to get smart. She went outside and called the press and some news crews. When they arrived, and all cameras were pointing at me, she asked, 'Mr. President, where are the UFOs that protect the White House?'"

[Laughter]

Me: "I nearly said, 'Go look for them on the roof.' But when I saw the news crews pointing their cameras at me, I knew the statement would be damaging, especially if I plan to run for a second term."

[Laughter]

Me: "So, I told the lady I had no idea what UFOs are but if they wanted to see HAND, they should go to the West Wing and check it out. All of them were so excited even though none of them knew what HAND stands for. As soon as they all left the room, I pulled the fire alarm, and everyone was forced to evacuate the White House."

[Laughter]

Me: "As the Secret Service were moving everyone out of the building, the smart lady who had asked me earlier about UFOs came to me and asked, 'Mr. President, what exactly does HAND stand for?' I replied, 'Oh! HAND stands for: Have A Nice Day.'"

[Laughter]

Me: "If you think you are smart, well, two can play at that game."

[Applause]

Me: "One American once said, 'In dogs we trust,' so the first thing I bought my family when we moved into the White House was a dog. I was excited because I'd never owned a dog before. But for the first three days, I noticed the dog didn't like me. That baffled me a lot, because Barbet water dogs are naturally friendly. I later found out that the dog didn't just hate me; he was a Republican."

[Laughter]

Me: "But that was cool; at least he made it to the White House."

[Laughter]

Me: "Yet, despite our political differences, the dog and I have some things in common. We are alike in complexion, and neither of us has a birth certificate."

[Laughter]

Me: "Okay, that was a joke. I have a birth certificate. It's at home if you want to see it."

[Laughter]

Me: "Sometimes, I have to be careful what I wish for. Even my own Secret Service agents scare me off sometimes. I'm sure you know, just like every other couple, the first lady and I make love at night."

I smiled.

Me: "Yes, we do. There's nothing secret about it. Catherine, Mariah, and Michael didn't drop from the sky."

[Applause]

Me: "And you know women are fond of screaming or saying something funny during copulation, like 'Help me' and so on and so forth."

[Laughter]

Me: "I guess the first lady must have used one of those funny words last night, because one of the Secret Service agents burst into our bedroom, turned on the light, and asked, 'Mr. President, is everything OKAY?' I said, 'Yes! Get the f@$k out of this room now before I lose my temper.'"

[Laughter]

Me: "He replied, 'Sir, you are sweating.' I said, 'DUDE, don't you have a wife?'"

[Laughter]

Me: "Again, he goes, 'Sir, I just want to make sure everything is fine.' I said, 'Then turn off the GOD-DAMN light and get lost.'"

[Laughter]

Me: "The press in this country is amazing."

[Applause]

Me: "Yes they are! Sometimes, they ask you questions they already know the answer to.

"The first interview I had with the press when I took office was terrific. The lady asked me a question. She said, 'Mr. President, considering the degree of backwardness the economy is facing right now, why are you so optimistic about the future? Why do you speak of so much hope in this time of depression?' So, I quoted what was written in John16:13: 'When the Spirit of truth comes, he will guide you into all truth. He will not speak on his own but will tell you what he has heard. He will tell you about the future.'" The press lady happened to be a Catholic, so she replied, 'Mr. President, the verse is speaking of the Holy Spirit. Are you claiming to be the Holy Spirit?' I replied, 'What do you think? When the father runs the office and, after his administration, he hands over the government to his son, after the son runs the office for eight years, you can bet the Holy Spirit is the next person the son will hand over power to.'"

[Laughter]

Me: "I was flabbergasted on my first day in office when I opened the son's administrative record. The first flaw I noticed was a huge mathematical error. No wonder the economy collapsed. George, how do you feed five thousand troops with two fishes and five loaves of bread and expect the economy to balance?"

[Laughter]

Me: "That was incredible! This guy is a genius!"

[Laughter]

Me: "He thinks he can destroy the temple in eight years and build it back in three days."

[Laughter]

Me: "Now that everyone is used to the son's miraculous behavior, they expect me to turn water to wine now that I'm president. Don't blame the Holy Spirit, blame the son."

[Applause]

Me: "I must confess, I went through a lot during my campaign. At one point, things got so odd that I didn't know who I was campaigning against: a plumber or a war hero."

[Laughter]

Me: "That was one hell of a campaign, Tim. How is the plumber doing?"

[Laughter]

Me: "I asked him after the campaign, 'Let's be honest, Tim. That plumber was a setup, wasn't it?' He replied, 'No, he wasn't.' I said, 'Yeah, I know, he's a plumber; he just doesn't have a plumber's license. That also makes me a perfect presidential candidate because I'm a US citizen, but I don't have a birth certificate.'"

[Laughter]

Me: "Was that the second time I said that?"

[Laughter]

Me: "Okay, if there's any press member in this room who has any doubt about my place of birth, you can follow me to the White House after the dinner. I brought my birth certificate with me to the White House when I moved there."

[Laughter]

Me: "On a more serious note, I'm proud of all of you for your commitment towards obtaining honest news and broadcasting the truth to the world.

You guys are one of the reasons why America is what it is today."

[Applause]

Me: "You took something as simple as the freedom of speech and turned it into accountability, a platform that exposes the good and bad behavior of the world, and with your unrelenting voice, each and every day, you've made it apparent to the world that you will not stop speaking until the world becomes a better place. Tonight, I want to say thank you to all of you. Thank you very much, everyone."

[A round of applause]

[Scene 91]

Two and a half months passed without any major problem, except a few inevitable heart droppers, you know, the protesters, the White House fence jumpers, and those unreasonable prank phone calls that kept the FBI and Secret Service up at night.

[Scene 92]

[June 27, around 5am]

I was sitting in my bedroom at the White House, waiting for the first lady to exit the shower so we could discuss her trip to Michael's school that day. The same day, at 4pm, I was scheduled to give a speech at Hampton College in Florida.

Air Force One wouldn't be leaving until 12pm; thus, I didn't know if the first lady wanted me to join the trip to Michael's school before heading to Florida.

I was talking to the first lady over the shower curtain when Michael bumped into the room and asked if I would attend the parents meeting at his school that day.

Me: "Your mum will attend the meeting. I have to prepare for my trip to Florida today."

Michael: "Aww. . . I thought you were coming. I've told all my friends, and they are all eager to meet you."

Me: "Sorry, not today. What's Mariah doing?"

Michael: "Getting ready for school."

Me: "Alright, tell her to join us in the dining room when she finishes. No one is skipping breakfast this morning."

[Scene 93]

At 6:30 am in the dining room, we all had a wonderful breakfast, and around 7:05 am, I watched the Secret Service drove Mariah to school.

At the same time, the Marine One helicopter was landing on the White House lawn. From the White House, I would be heading straight to Andrews Air Force Base in Maryland, where Air force One was waiting.

Mariah had celebrated her fourteenth birthday a week earlier and gotten a puppy as a birthday gift. That morning, she wanted to take the dog to school, but I didn't allow her. That was the reason I specifically followed her outside to make sure she and the Secret Service didn't sneak the dog in their car with them. The last time, Michael had taken the dog to school, and the next day I had to answer all sorts of unreasonable questions from the press.

I stood at the doorway for some minutes, reading a newspaper I had picked up from the floor before going back to my room to finish my preparations.

[Scene 94]

When the first lady and Michael were ready to leave, I gave her a kiss and clapped Michael on the head.

Me: "See you guys tomorrow."

Michael: "Ok, Dad."

I was the last person to leave the White House that morning.

[Scene 95]

Mariah's school was approximately a mile away from the White House. It was partially visible if you stood on the White House roof.

From the window of Marine One, I looked in the direction of her school as we made our way to Andrews Air Force Base in Maryland.

[Scene 96]

It was around 11:45 am when Marine One touched down at Andrews Air Force Base.

I had planned to address some of the staff at the base before boarding Air Force One. I changed my mind when I remembered the vice president had given a speech there the day before. I boarded the plane as soon as I landed at the base.

[Scene 97]

Tired and hungry, I ordered a cheeseburger and fries and went straight to bed after I finished eating. Before I went to my room, I told the staff on the plane not to wake me up until we arrived in Florida.

The flight time from Andrews AFB to Florida was approximately two hours. I thought I should be able to get at least an hour of rest.

[Scene 98]

I hadn't spent a minute on the bed when I heard a heavy knock on my door. It was as if the person at the door was going to force his way in. I didn't know what to think when I opened it.

My national security advisor, James, walked into

my private room in a hurry and found himself a seat.

James: "Mr. President, we have a situation."

Me: "What's going on, James?"

James: "Sir, where's your TV remote?"

James found the remote and turned the TV Channel to CNN.

Me: "Is that Bronx Reynolds? That's Mariah's school. James, what happened there?"

James: "There was a report of an active shooter at the school some moments ago."

James's, Air Force One's, and my phone all rang at the same time. There was another knock on the door. The press secretary, Shawn, entered the room.

Shawn: "Mr. President, something bad has happened. I just received a confirmed report that Bronx Reynolds High School is under attack.

A couple of people inside the school have been shot, including Secret Service agents. Sir, this is not a joke. Bronx Reynolds is under attack."

Me: "Take me back to Washington."

James: "Mr. President, I think it's best if you–"

Me: "TURN THIS GODDAMN PLANE ARO-UND NOW."

James: "Yes, sir."

James telephoned the Air Force One pilot.

Pilot: "Just making sure, sir. You're asking me to return to Andrews Air Force Base. Is that correct?"

James: "Yes, that's a direct order from the president."

Pilot: "Copy that. Change of plan acknowledged. Air Force One is returning to base."

The vice president, Paul, got on the phone with me.

Paul: "How far away are you from Andrews?"

Me: "We should be touching down in ten minutes. Paul, where's my family? I've been trying to reach Mariah and her Secret Service agents. No one is answering."

Paul: "Michael and the first lady are here with me at the White House. The Secretary of Defense is on a chopper back to Washington. Only a few students got out of the school before the incident started. Mariah isn't one of them. Every branch of law enforcement in the nation is surrounding that school as we speak."

Me: "Paul, how did this happen?"

Paul: "I wish I could tell you, Mr. President. The Secret Service director is also here. He couldn't reach any of the agents with Mariah. The last report we received confirmed that everyone left inside the school is being held hostage."

Me: "This is ridiculous. How the hell did they get pass the Secret Service?"

Paul: "I don't know. The Secret Service director is here if you want to talk to him."

Me: "Tell him to meet me at the West Wing. I want to see the Secretary of Defense, the major generals and every goddamn personal official who can answer my questions; I want all of them in the West Wing basement now."

[Scene 99]

A bunch of official black SUVs raced towards the White House.

[Scene 100]

A CRN female reporter was speaking live outside Bronx Reynolds.

Reporter: "I'm here on 14th street and Pennsylvania Avenue at the nation's capital, and if you look behind me, you will see a lot of police and FBI activities surrounding Bronx Reynolds High School. That's the school where Mariah, one of President Bull's daughters, currently attends.

"According to eyewitness accounts, around 11:15 this morning, about seven to eight gunmen holding powerful assault rifles entered the school and opened fire. We don't know if anyone inside the building is dead.

"One of the students who managed to escape told reporters that a gunfight broke out between the gunmen and the Secret Service agents protecting Mariah. We don't know the condition of the students or Secret Service agents inside the building. However, one thing is certain, if the threat inside the school has been completely eliminated by the Secret Service agents inside the building, they should be bringing people out now.

"As you can see, SWAT teams are positioned everywhere around the school, and some are just arriving. If you look at the roof of that tall building to my right and also the one on my left, you will see about seven to ten snipers pointing their guns at the school building.

"All we can do now is wait and pray that every student and good guy inside Bronx Reynolds comes out alive. We will continue to bring you more updates as we learn more about the incident."

******

Cataphrase D

"You've taken the first step towards success the day you stop following them and decide to lead."

—Teni A.

[Scene 101]

I arrived at the White House on Marine One, which landed on the lawn.

[Scene 102]

[Inside the White House]

The White House chief of staff, Chucks, met with me in the hallway. We walked to the Situation Room.

Chuck: "Welcome, Mr. President. Please, everyone, move out of the way. The president is not answering questions at this time."

Me: "Chuck, where's everyone?"

Chuck: "The conference room, sir."

[Scene 103]

Chuck and I arrived at the situation Room.

Me (to everyone): "What happened?"

FBI Director (John): "Around 11 this morning, about eight to nine gunmen forced their way inside Bronx Reynolds High School. About 156 students were inside the school at the time. Only fifty-two students escaped. The rest are still inside.

"One of the school guards who checked in the terrorists said they were dressed like contractors and presented IDs that corresponded with the company that usually works on the school's garden.

"Three Secret Service agents are confirmed shot. The rest of the agents were outside when the incident started. They couldn't make their way in."

Secret Service Director (Collins): "According to Secret Service protocol, sir, unless there's an emergency, only three agents are allowed inside Mariah's classroom at a time."

John: "I have two of the FBI's best negotiators on the scene. On the screen behind you is a visual of every corner of the school. We've positioned snipers to cover every window and door that leads in and out of the building.

"So far, we've only identify one of the gunmen. His name is Ziad Mohan.

"Ziad is thirty-seven. Nationality is Saudi Arabian. He arrived in the United States in early April four years ago and settled in Brooklyn.

"He worked at various carry-out restaurants in the last two years, but he is currently registered as a cab driver. His last known address is 1105 Cherry Court Road, Apartment 9, in Harlem. There are hundreds of police officers and FBI agents searching that apartment as we speak."

Me: "What about the rest of them? Have any of them talked? What did they want? Who is their leader?"

John: "We've been trying to reach them, but we have not yet established communications. The FBI agents on the scene are looking at the cameras inside the school building now to find out what's going on there.

"Some of the cameras inside the school were destroyed by the terrorists. As far as the identities of the other terrorists, we can only hope the search at Ziad's house yields vital clues as to the identity of the remaining terrorists."

Vice President: "Mr. President, I think it's best if

you stay with your family upstairs."

Me: "Where are the first lady and Michael?"

Collins: "They're in the East Wing. I've sent extra Secret Service agents down to Florida to make sure Catherine is fine."

Me: "The Secret Service agents staying with Mariah, what type of guns are they armed with?"

Collins: "They're armed with the SIG Sauer P226. The agents with the big guns usually stay outside or inside the armored SUV."

Me: "The terrorists, what type of guns are they armed with?"

John: "From what I saw earlier in the surveillance video of a hallway inside the school, two of the three masked men captured on tape were holding what appeared to be Mac10s. I couldn't identify what type of gun the third masked man was holding."

Me: "Where's the surveillance video? I want to see

it. How long is the CCTV footage?"

John: "Twenty-one seconds. Over here, sir."

Me (while watching the video): "That's a German made armor-piercing MP 40 9mm pistol. First introduced during World War II."

John: "The ATF approved sales of the MP 40 in the United States last year."

Major General: "The P226 carried by the Secret Service agents staying with Mariah is no match to the MP 40."

[Scene 104]

[Command post outside Bronx Reynolds]

An FBI negotiator tried to call the principal's office at Bronx Reynolds.

[Phone ringing . . . Call disconnected]

FBI Negotiator (on the radio): "All snipers, please report your visual. Do you see any movement at the windows?"

Sniper One: "Negative."

Sniper Two: "Negative."

Sniper Three: "No visual, I got nothing."

Sniper Four: "Negative. No movement."

[Short silence]

FBI Negotiator: "Sniper Five, please report your visual."

Sniper Five: "Hold on. I've got something. I see movement at the window facing the tennis court. Someone just tossed out a white sheet of paper."

FBI Negotiator: "Copy that. I'm sending four men to pick it up."

[Scene 105]

Four SWAT officers approached the tennis court, guns drawn. One was speaking on the radio.

SWAT Officer: "Command, I see movement at the windows here. One boogie is holding a hostage at gunpoint. It looks like he's trying to tell us something. *Son of a bitch*! The hostage is wrapped in explosives."

FBI Negotiator: "Alpha Team, do not engage the boogie. Just pick up the note and step back. I repeat, do not engage."

SWAT Officer: "Copy that. We are stepping back. I think I recognize that hostage girl."

FBI Negotiator: "I hope it's not who I'm thinking."

[Scene 106]

Alpha Team leader arrived at the FBI command post with a note in hand. He read it and then turned to another FBI agent inside the command post.

FBI Negotiator: "Carl, I want to know the name and address associated with this number. Every call in and out from the past six months, I want to see them now.

FBI Agent: "I already did. The number is registered to Bronx Reynolds High School. The same one we are dealing with."

[Scene 107]

John received a cell phone call at the Situation Room.

John: "FBI Director. Who's speaking?"

FBI Negotiator: "This is Command Post 7. I just received a note from the terrorist. I'm faxing it to you right away."

Someone in the Situation Room brought a note to John.

John (reading the terrorist note in front of everyone there): "To whom it may concern. I've taken red and white hostages. Most importantly, I have the blue hostage. If you want the red and white hostages, tell the FBI to call me. But if you want to see the blue hostage alive again, tell the president to call me at 606-333-5555. This is war; don't underestimate what I can do."

Vice President: "He refers to the hostages in color. Why?"

Major General: "Vice President, the red, white, and blue represents the American flag. The colors red and white stand for Americans or an American property.

"The color blue means an important American or an important American asset. Good examples of when blue is used include for a United States passport, Air Force One, the boys in blue, members of the Navy, and, most important of all, the United States president and his family members. Mr. Vice President, that blue hostage stands for Mariah, the president's daughter."

Me: "John, give me that number."

Secretary of Defense: "No, Mr. President, you can't call the terrorists. That's the job of the FBI negotiator. I know you're upset at the moment, but the United States president does not call a terrorist when he needs help."

Me (angrily): "So, who does he call, you? The Chinese president? When Americans need help, they call on their president. But when the president needs help, WHO THE HELL DOES HE CALL?"

Secretary of Defense: "He calls on God."

Me (still angry): "And if God doesn't respond in time?"

Major General: "He calls on the Marines."

[Short silence]

I left the Situation Room to join my family upstairs.

Secretary of State (to Major General): "Are you suggesting that the president deploy special forces inside the United States?"

Major General: "I'm not suggesting. I was trying

to outline the options available to the president in time of war or public danger."

Secretary of State: "You call this a war? This is just a hostage situation, for God's sake. This is not the first time we've experienced a hostage situation in America. War! I don't see rockets falling from the sky or bombs bursting in the air."

Major General: "When are we going to finally sit down and listen to the story that history is trying to tell us?

"Before Pearl Harbor was attacked, we were warned. But we waited until we saw it happen before we took action. Before the Twin Towers fell, we were warned, yet we waited until we saw it happen before we declared war.

"Again, we have been warned. Do we have to wait until Bronx Reynolds starts falling and hundreds of Americans die before we declare war on a terrorist who has declared war on us? The man clearly said in his note that this is war.

"Don't get me wrong, I'm not asking the president to invade a high school with armored tanks and cruise missiles. Declaring war in this sense simply means let's use our military resources to defend Americans."

Attorney General: "The president can only deploy military forces in times of war. I agree with the Secretary of State. This is just a hostage situation. We should allow the FBI to handle it."

Major General: "I would have also agreed except for the fact that the terrorist mentioned in his note that this is an act of war, and—"

A phone call interrupted the conversation. John picked up the call and placed it on speaker.

John: "John speaking."

FBI Negotiator (on the phone): "This is Command Post 7. I have the terrorist leader on the line. He refused to speak to me. He insisted he wants to talk to someone who is not a negotiator."

John: "Put him through."

[Call transferred]

John: "Hello, my name is John. I'm the FBI director. Who am I speaking with?"

Terrorist Leader (on the phone): "It doesn't matter. My name is not important. Now, listen to what I'm about to say. I know you're eager to talk to me. You want to know what I want. I don't want anything from you. I'm not a beggar, I'm a soldier. However, at 6 pm today, I want you to deliver four large pepperoni pizzas here, and in return, I'll give you four hostages."

John: "That's not a problem, I can get you those pizzas by 6 pm. How are the hostages doing?"

Terrorist Leader: "They are all here with me."

John: "Good. Do you need more pizza for the hostages? I can add more to the pizzas if you want. Hello? Hello? Hello? Damn. He hung up."

Secretary of State: "He's asking for food? What kind of terrorist is this?"

John: "That's not bad: four large pepperoni pizzas

for four hostages. That sound like a good start to me."

[5:50 pm]

John (calling the terrorist leader): "Hello, this is John, FBI director. Your pepperoni pizza is ready. Where do you want me to deliver it?"

Terrorist Leader: "Send four unarmed men to the door by the tennis courts. Let each man carry one box of pizza. The four hostages I promised to release will be at the door by 6pm."

John: "Alright, thanks. Is there anything else you want me to do for you at this time? Hello? Hello? Alright, he hung up again."

[Scene 108]

[6pm]

Four unarmed men approached one of the entrances to Bronx Reynolds. Each of them carried one large box of pepperoni pizza. Once they dropped the pizzas at the doorstep, the door opened slightly, and four dead bodies were tossed outside. The four unarmed men each carried one body back to the FBI command post outside Bronx Reynolds.

[Scene 109]

[6:05 pm in the Situation Room]

John (to the terrorist leader on the phone): "You promised to deliver four hostages to me; you didn't tell me they were dead."

Terrorist Leader: "You didn't ask. But that's fine, because now I know you are not a negotiator."

John: "How are you so sure of that?"

Terrorist Leader: "Because if you were a negotiator, you would have asked if the hostages I promised to release were dead or alive. Besides, I don't eat pepperoni; it's against my religion. If I'm hungry, there are enough food and drinks here in the vending machines to last me for days. John, you can call me Ghazi. In Arabic, it means 'Warrior.' I'll talk to you again at midnight."

[Call disengaged]

Secretary of State (to John): "All right. That's one hell of a start. Have your men identified those dead bodies?"

Collins: "We have. Three of them were the agents that stayed with Mariah inside her classroom. The fourth guy is the security guard that was standing at the school entrance."

Vice President: "John, who is your best negotiator?"

John: "He's at the hostage scene."

Vice President: "I need him here now."

John: "He tried earlier to start the negotiation; the terrorist won't talk to him."

Vice President: "I don't need him to talk to the terrorist. I need him to instruct you on how to negotiate when you start talking to the terrorist again."

[Short silence]

[Scene 110]

A black FBI SUV raced down Pennsylvania Avenue towards the White House.

[Scene 111]

The FBI negotiator from Command Post 7 arrived at the Situation Room.

FBI Negotiator: "We just completed the search at Ziad's apartment. Our boys found traces of explosives residue inside one of the rooms. The record of the apartment showed it was leased to Ziad Talim and Hammed Bohan.

"I did a background check on Hammed Bohan. He owns another house in Florida. CIA records show Hammed is related to Bin Laden."

Vice President: "Does Hammed have any other family member inside the United States? If he does, where are they?"

FBI Negotiator: "This is where things get interesting. Four months ago, Hammed's wife and two kids living in Saudi Arabia applied for

American visas.

"Two weeks before their interview at the America Embassy, the 707 bill took effect. When the embassy discovered that Hammed's wife and kids were related to Bin Laden, their visa was immediately denied.

"We traced the tag on the van parked outside Bronx Reynolds. It was rented out to Hammed Bohan seven days ago."

Vice President: "Now we know who Ghazi is. His real name is Hammed Bohan. He's not a warrior, he's a coward."

FBI Negotiator: "Ghazi, is that what he called himself?"

John: "Yes, he wants me to call him Ghazi. In Arabic, it means warrior. He'll call again at midnight."

Secretary of State (to FBI negotiator): "When he calls at midnight, should we refer to him as Ghazi or his real name?"

FBI Negotiator (to John): "Ask him if you should call him Ghazi or Hammed Bohan. When you call someone who is trying to remain anonymous by their full name, they will momentarily release their tension and open up to you a bit. He's more likely to hang up the phone when you ask him the question, but don't worry; he'll call you back."

[Scene 112]

[Outside Bronx Reynolds]

The second FBI negotiator at Command Post 7 was speaking to one of the teachers who had escaped from Bronx Reynolds before the incident started.

Second Negotiator: "Ma'am, one of the students we interviewed said you were at Mariah's class when the incident started. Can you tell us how the incident unfolded?"

Teacher: "It was horrible. I was going from classroom to classroom, telling students about the new novels that were delivered to our library this morning.

"Before I entered Mariah's classroom, the Secret Service agent at the door checked my ID. I'd only spoken one or two words to the students when I heard the sound of a gunshot.

"I turned in the direction of the sound and saw the Secret Service agent at the door lying on the floor. Four gunmen walked into the classroom and started shooting. One of the remaining Secret Service agents managed to wrestle some students out through the exit door.

"The other agent wasn't so lucky. He was making his way to the door with Mariah when he was shot. The first Secret Service agent came back and exchanged fire with the masked gunmen.

"I managed to crawl out of the exit door and ran to the gym before jumping outside through the window."

Second Negotiator: "How many gunmen did you see in total?"

Teacher: "Four of them entered the classroom. On my way to the gym, I saw another two gunmen standing at the exit doors."

Second Negotiator: "So, you saw six gunmen in total?"

Another FBI agent entered the command post and interrupted the conversation.

FBI Agent: "Guys, there's another problem."

Second Negotiator: "Ma'am, thanks for your co-operation. You are free to go."

The teacher exited the command post.

FBI Agent: "A bomb just went off in Hammed's house in Florida. Five FBI agents who entered the house to execute a search are dead. Seven police officers standing outside were seriously wounded. Two of them died before paramedics arrived."

Second Negotiator: "I'm calling the White House."

[Scene 113]

[9:15 pm. Situation Room]

An FBI agent at Command Post 7 was on the phone with John.

John (on his cell phone): "Hello. . .Jesus... Just now? Thanks."

Secretary of State: "John, who's that?"

John: "A bomb just went off inside Hammed's house in Florida, killing five FBI agents and two police officers."

Vice President: "Screw midnight; call that son of a bitch now."

FBI Negotiator (to John): "You have to be calm when talking to him. And ask him first if you should call him Ghazi or Hammed Bohan. I'll instruct you on what to say or ask. When he asks you questions, I'll write the answer on this board."

John telephoned Bronx Reynolds. The terrorist leader answered the call.

Terrorist Leader: "John, it's not midnight. Why are you calling me?"

John: "I know. But first, Ghazi, I have a question to ask you. Do you want me to continue calling you

Ghazi, or would you prefer if I call you Hammed Bohan? Hello? Hello? He hung up."

FBI Negotiator: "Don't worry, give him some time. He'll call back."

Five minutes later, the situation room phone rang. John picked it up.

John: "John speaking."

Hammed: "What else do you know about me?"

John: "Your house in Florida, a bomb went off there some minutes ago killing five people. Why didn't you tell me about the bomb?"

Hammed: "Why didn't you ask me if my house was safe before you sent your men inside?"

John: "How am I supposed to know you have a bomb in your house?"

Hammed: "*ASK.* I told you in my note not to underestimate what I can do. This is war."

The FBI negotiator was showing questions and answers to John. He wrote: *Ask if there are more bombs you should know about.*

John (still speaking to Hammed on the phone): "Are there more bombs I should know about?"

Hammed: "Now you are asking the right question. I meant to tell you about the bombs when I called at midnight. But since you've asked, I also want something in return."

John: "What do you want?"

Hammed: "Tell the president and all members of Congress to bring my family to America. In return, I'll give you everything that's left and the hostages. John, that's a small request compared to what I'm offering you. Give me this, and I'll give you everything."

John: "Your demand is not impossible, but it's highly improbable. We can arrange to fly you out of the country to join your family and give you some money."

Hammed: "Money? Tell me, John, how much money do you have? If you and every member of the United States Congress is for sale, I can buy all of you. Now, back to what I was saying. What time is it, John?"

John: "It's 10:45."

Hammed: "You don't have much time left, John. Let me know when you are ready to make a deal."

[Call disengaged]

Vice President: "His demand is unreasonable. I would have suggested we offer him some money in exchange for the bombs, but he talks like he is Bill Gates."

CIA Director: "He's right. Trying to offer him money will be like trying to offer Bin Laden money to surrender when he was alive. Hammed is a cousin to Bin Laden, and if you all remember who Bin Laden was the son of, you will understand what I'm talking about. It's where you get your oil from.

No one in that family is worth less than ten million dollars."

John: "No wonder the police dogs couldn't detect the bomb in his house in Florida. The explosive residue we found in his house is an expensive military grade A, an SSP value. Only the military has access to that type of bomb, and only a dog that is trained with that type of explosive can detect it."

Vice President: "Director, I want every record of this guy's life, now. His friends, where he shops, if he had a job, who employed him, everywhere he's visited, bank transfers, phone records, and internet records.

"Check every surveillance camera around his house, train station, bus station, airport, and find out every state he's visited since 707 took effect. John, put every transportation station in the metropolitan area on high alert. If this son of a bitch has another bomb somewhere, I want to know before the sun rises tomorrow. John, call him back now and ask him about the bombs again."

John: "And if he insists on his demand?"

Vice President: "Lie to him. I don't care. Just make him talk."

FBI Negotiator: "We can't lie to him. That will only make things worse. Trust is a key factor when you are negotiating with a terrorist. If we lose that key, we lose access to the mind of the terrorist. What I suggest we do is tell him we'll deliver his message to the president tonight."

Vice President (to John)**:** "Call him."

John telephoned Bronx Reynolds. Hammed answered the call.

Hammed: "John, do you have my family?"

John: "Not yet. Even if I travel at the speed of light, that won't be possible tonight. But I can promise you one thing: if you tell me about the rest of the bombs, I'll pass your request along to the president tonight. That's a promise, and I'll keep that promise."

Hammed: "I don't have any more bombs."

John: "You told me earlier that you meant to tell me about the bombs when you called at midnight."

Hammed: "Yes, I was referring to the bomb that went off in my house in Florida."

The FBI negotiator showed a note to John: *Ask him about everything that's left. He mentioned something in reference to that earlier.*

John (to Hammed): "What about everything you have left? You mentioned something in reference to that earlier."

Hammed: "What time is it, John?"

John: "It's 11:09. Why?"

Hammed: "I own another house here in Washington, DC. By 12:30am, the house will be ready for war. When it starts, no one can stop it. No one in the vicinity would escape it. Not even I, you, the president, or these hostages. Only a person who is trained for war can stop it before it starts."

John: "Where is your house in Washington located?"

Hammed: "Call my cell phone. I left it there."

[Call disengaged]

John: "Hello? Hello? He's out."

Secretary of State (to CIA director): "What number is registered in his name?"

CIA Director: "He has two lines registered under his name. One of the lines was open just recently. No in-calls and no out-calls yet. The line is still active."

Vice President: "Call the number."

FBI Negotiator: "No, Mr. Vice President. We can't call the number."

Vice President: "Why?"

FBI Negotiator: "Even when a captor is giving you something in return, you still have to think twice before you do what he asks you to do. If the phone is connected to an explosive, calling the number will set it off. That's probably why there's no in-call or out-call in the phone records. I suggest we trace the number instead of calling it."

Vice President (to CIA director): "Trace the number. How much time do we have left?"

Secretary of State: "It's 11:15pm. We have about an hour and fifteen minutes remaining."

[A minute later]

CIA Director: "I got it. The cell phone is located at 5052 Ostrich Drive, southeast DC."

Vice President: "I want everyone in that vicinity evacuated right away. I want that house thoroughly searched. Guys, we don't have much time. Let's do it."

Major General: "Mr. Vice President, I think this situation is more than what the police or the FBI can handle. If you remember, the terrorist mentioned that only a person trained for war can stop this madness. We couldn't find the bomb in his house in Florida because the men we deployed didn't have the training required to find it.

"If the bomb in Hammed's house turns out to be another SSP value or higher, no dogs in any of our law enforcement agencies can sniff it out, except the ones we've trained for war. And God forbid, if it turns out to be of a higher value, no one within a five-yard radius will survive the blast.

"Mr. Vice President, when a terrorist takes Americans hostage, including a member of the first family, kills Secret Service agents, police officers, and FBI agents, and declares war on America with dangerous weapons of war, I'm afraid to tell you this, Mr. Vice President, but if you ask me, I would say America is under attack."

Vice President: "Major, put the president on the phone now."

A call went out to the East Wing. I answered the call. The major general was on the line, and I put him on speaker phone. He explained the current situation to me.

Me: "Major, what other options do we have?"

Major General: "We have no other options, Mr. President, and we are running out of time. The only way to solve this problem is to deploy military resources, and it has to happen now."

Me (to the Secretary of Defense): "Ryan."

Secretary of Defense: "I'm here, Mr. President."

Me: "How would I explain to Congress that I deployed the military to resolve a hostage situation?"

Secretary of Defense: "Mr. President, this no longer a hostage situation. This is an act of war. In a situation like this, the AUMF authorization act gives you the power to use all necessary and appropriate military force to defend and protect Americans here at home and abroad. Mr. President, we have approximately one hour and five minutes remaining."

Me: "Major, are you still there?"

Major General: "Yes, I'm still here, Mr. President."

Me: "Good. When the president needs help, who does he call?"

Major General: "He calls on God."

Me: "And if God doesn't respond him in time?"

Major General: "He calls on the Marines."

Me: "General, how soon can you deploy military resources to that house?"

Major General: "As soon as you give the orders, Mr. President."

Me: "Do it, now."

Major General: "Orders acknowledged."

The major general hung up and called the nearest Marine base.

Major General: "Echo 5, this is the United States Marine General Escobar 5550, Star Freedom. Tag, Oscar. Red Cobra, Eagle One. Location 5052 Ostrich Drive, southeast Washington, DC. Possible threat, SSP explosive or higher value. Asset needed,

Grade 10 sniffing dogs, Grade 10 bomb squad. Marine officers should be equipped in M3 gear. Use CH-47f Chinook to maximize speed. Time is paramount. Location has no landing zone. Fast rope drop on target."

Cataphrase E

"With my level of anxiety, there's no way I
can pass a polygraph test."

—Teni A.

[Scene 114]

Marine Officer (at Andy Base): "Roger that, Star Freedom. Orders acknowledged. We're on our way. ETA to target: fifteen minutes."

[Scene 115]

Four CH-47f Chinooks carrying forty equipped Marine officers and ten Marine German Shepherds flew across the sky. They headed towards Hammed's house in DC at high speed.

[Scene 116]

I entered the Situation Room. The time was 12:01 am.

Secretary of Defense: "Mr. President, the Marines just arrived at Hammed's house. We can see everything they are doing on this screen."

[Scene 117]

[Hammed's house in Washington, DC]

Forty equipped Marines rappelled out of four CH-47f Chinooks into the compound.

Ten Marine SSP bomb squad experts accompanied by ten Grade 10 German Shepherds cautiously made their way into Hammed's house.

The M3 gear they wore was some of the best military grade gear in the world. It provided full-body protection from fire, gas, and biochemical attacks. It also included gas mask, night vision goggles, and a portable oxygen tank.

[Scene 118]

With military-style precision, they searched every room in the house for explosives and other threats. Three of the dogs, which were specialized in biochemical and gas sniffing, sensed an odor and traced the source to the roof of the house.

[Scene 119]

One of the dogs sat when it zeroed in on a cell phone attached to a barrel.

For clarification, a Marine K9 expert uses his fingers to communicate with the dog. Each finger he raises represents a different gas or biochemical weapon. When the Marine K9 expert raises the finger that corresponds with the gas the dog detected, the dog will bark twice.

The Marine raised his thumb for VX gas, but the dog didn't respond. The second finger he raised was his index finger, for mushroom gas, but the dog didn't respond. The third finger he raised was his middle finger, for sarin gas, and the dog barked twice. The Marine officer called in the situation immediately.

[Scene 120]

The Marine officer on the roof, Bravo Echo 5, got the major general in the situation Room on the radio.

Bravo Echo: "Star Freedom this is Bravo Echo 5. Sarin war gas is detected. The gas is contained inside a barrel on the roof of the house. Mode of trigger: cell phone call. Should I proceed with deactivation?"

Secretary of Defense: "Not yet. Stand by."

Secretary of Defense (to major general): "Major, if that gas mistaken goes off, how many fatalities are we looking at?"

One of the FBI's chemical experts looking at the barrel from the CCTV screen in the situation Room interrupted.

Chemical Expert: "From the size of that barrel, every life form within a five-mile radius will die within twenty-four hours."

Vice President: "Major."

Major General: "Bravo Echo 5, how long will it take to deactivate the bomb?"

Bravo Echo: "Five, maybe seven minutes. Let's just hope the phone doesn't ring before then."

Major General: "Bravo Echo, you can proceed with the deactivation."

Bravo Echo: "Roger that."

Secretary of Defense: "Mr. President, we need to move you and your remaining family to a safe zone in Boston."

Me: "Forget it. I'm not leaving Mariah. Has the terrorist spoken? What does he want?"

John: "He wants you and the members of Congress to bring his family to the United States."

Me: "So, that's what all this is about? The 707 law is that why he's doing this?"

John: "I believe so, Mr. President."

[12:26 am]

Bravo Echo interrupted the conversation over the speaker phone.

Bravo Echo (over the radio): "Star Freedom, the package is secured."

Major General: "Good job, Bravo Echo. You're cleared to transport the package to MH.

some chemical experts are waiting there to rece-
the package."

Me: "How did sarin gas gets into the hands of a
terrorist inside the United States?"

Major General: "The last known attack involving
sarin gas happened in Tokyo. With enough money
and the right scientists, if—"

A phone call interrupted the conversation.

[12:30 am]

John answered the call.

John: "John speaking."

Hammed: "I planned for everything to end at this
time, but since all of us are still here, I guess you
found the barrel. John, another war has just begun.
If the president doesn't repeal the 707 bill by 6am,
I'll release one red and white hostage every hour
until I release the blue hostage."

John: "Dead or alive?"

Hammed: "Dead."

[Call disengaged]

Secretary of State: "He's asking us to repeal our constitution?"

Me: "He's asking for trouble. What do we know about the number and positions of the terrorists inside the building?"

John: "According to one eyewitness, there are nine to ten terrorists inside the building. We have a CCTV video feed from all the cameras inside the school except the indoor basketball gym and the lunch room. I believe they destroyed the cameras in those rooms. Here's the map of the building interior."

John stood up and showed everyone the map of the school's interior on a big screen.

John: "Here and there is where the cameras are knocked out. I believe they are holding the hostages in one of those rooms."

Me: "So, we have the estimated number of terrorists, we know what type of guns three of them are holding, and we know where they are holding the hostages. Do we have a plan to storm the building?"

John: "I can have three FBI SWAT teams storm the building from the three main entrances. With speed and surprise, we can defeat them. But there's a problem. The blue hostage is wrapped in explosives. If the explosives attached to Mariah are the same quality as the bomb that went off in Florida, Mr. President, not only are we looking at total destruction of the building, but everything around Bronx Reynolds would be destroyed."

Vice President: "Mr. President, you have to go back to the East Wing now. The first lady has been trying to reach you. The FBI will continue with the situation from here."

Me: "I should. Major, Mr. Vice President, I need both of you to come with me to the East Wing."

[Scene 121]

[East Wing]

Me: "Major, what time is it?"

Major General: "It's 3:55am."

Me: "This asshole promised to start releasing bodies by 6. We have no reason to believe he won't keep his promise."

Major General: "We can tell the FBI negotiator to stall him a little to buy more time for the assault."

Me: "No more negotiation, Major. Before I became president, I took an oath to defend the Constitution of the United States to the best of my ability."

"Major, where is that thing we tested at Area 51 a month after I became marine general? The XRBM Jezebel, the one we launched the same day we launched Hell. Where is it?"

Vice President (interrupting the conversation): "Mr. President, what is 'Hell'?"

Major General: "It's classified."

Vice President: "Classified, my ass. The only thing that's classified is what we don't know exists. I'm the vice president of the United States, Major, what the heck is Hell?"

Me: "It's a bomb. Do you remember the Russians' ICBM nicknamed 'Satan'?"

Vice President: "Yeah, what about it?"

Me: "Just as God created hell to destroy Satan, the bomb Hell was created in response to the Satan threat. One United States ICBM nicknamed 'Hell' can destroy a planet the size of the moon. A nation can withstand Satan, but no nation can withstand hell. Six of them are carried by three of our submarines somewhere in the depths of the Pacific and Atlantic oceans."

Vice President: "Six? Jesus . . . I thought we agreed to dispose of all these weapons a long time ago. What about the XRBM Jezebel? What does that have to do with the hostage situation?"

Me: "You're about to find out. Major, what are the

procedures I have to follow if I want to use the XRBM Jezebel?"

Major General: "Mr. President, Jezebel is a weapon of war. To use the weapon, all you have to do is declare war, and I'll have it ready for use anywhere in the world in less than ten minutes."

Me: "I already did, Major. Go and prepare the weapon."

[Scene 122]

The Major General exited the White house in a Marine chopper.

XRBM Jezebel is a powerful, dangerous, and advanced high-technological military laser weapon. It operates the same way a sniper and his spotter operate. But unlike a sniper's bullet, which stops when it hits a solid object, the XRBM laser can cut through solid objects like metal, rock, and walls to eliminate its target at the speed of light.

Just as a bullet fired by a sniper travels in a straight line, when the XRBM Jezebel laser is fired at a target, the beam cuts a clean hole through whatever is in its path up to two miles away.

Here is where the XR comes in. The XR in the XRBM stands for X-Radar. It works just like an X-ray machine. It's used to see the position of a target inside a building or an opaque object.

The BM stands for an invisible non-lethal ordinary laser beam that is used to mark a target for the lethal Jezebel laser. The person using the invisible BM laser to mark a target must wear night vision goggles to see the BM laser beam.

[Scene 123]

[Outside Bronx Reynolds]

Marine helicopters and various military vehicles arrived outside the school.

[Scene 124]

CRN Reporter: "Folks, I'm not sure what's going on. You can see to my right some military vehicles arriving at the scene. It appears as if they are getting ready to evacuate everyone in the area. I don't know if there's a bomb threat. The soldiers coming out of those Humvees look like bomb squads.

[Scene 125]

[Inside the command post outside Bronx Reynolds]

A Marine officer entered the post.

Marine Officer: "I'm Captain Sean. I have direct orders from the United States president. The military will be taking over this situation from here. You have less than ten minutes to remove your belongings; we will be evacuating everyone from this area momentarily."

[Scene 126]

[Situation Room]

[5:42 am]

The conference phone in the situation room rang. John answered it.

John: "John speaking."

Hammed (over the phone): "Has the president

repealed the bill?"

John: "Not yet. I need more time to talk to the president. However—"

[Call disengaged]

John: "Hello? Hello? Damn."

[Scene 127]

[Outside Bronx Reynolds]

[5:45 am]

A female hostage exited Bronx Reynolds building alone, with her hands tied.

Female Hostage (screaming): "Please, help! Help me, please. . . ."

[Scene 128]

[Inside Command Post 7]

Captain Sean (on the radio)**:** "Bravo 3, secure that hostage now."

Bravo 3 Leader: "Roger that."

[Scene 129]

Four Marine officers moved towards the female hostage, their guns drawn.

Bravo 3 Leader (yelling)**:** "BOMB! Everyone, move back. There's a bomb strapped to her."

The female hostage didn't know what to do; thus, she ran towards a group of people. As everyone was running away from her, a Marine officer ran towards the female hostage and dropped her to the ground. The bomb went off, killing both of them.

[Scene 130]

[6:05 am]

I entered the Situation Room.

Me: "What happened?"

John: "A bomb just went off outside Bronx Reynolds, killing a hostage and a Marine."

The conference phone in the situation room rang. John answered it.

John: "John."

Hammed: "Has the president repealed the law?"

John: "Why did you kill that woman?"

Hammed: "I told you we are at war. You have another hour, John. This time, I'll be releasing two white hostages."

[Call disengaged]

Secretary of Defense: "Mr. President."

There was a short silence before I replied.

Me: "For the first time in the history of the United States, a member of the first family is held hostage. In less than twenty-four hours, five FBI agents, three Secret Service agents, two police officers, one

Marine officer, and two civilians have been killed by a terrorist inside the United States who has declared war on us because of our Constitution. Gentlemen, this madness is over."

I got on the phone with the marine general.

Marine General (on the phone): "Mr. President."

Me: "Execute the plan."

[Scene 131]

[Outside Bronx Reynolds]

Shortly after the explosion outside Bronx Reynolds High School, the area was evacuated of every civilian.

Seventeen Green Dragons, advanced military tactical vehicles, each carrying a BM and Jezebel, positioned themselves one hundred feet from the high school.

Another seventeen Rainbows, smaller advanced military tactical vehicles, each carrying an XR, were positioned fifty feet directly in front of each vehicle carrying a BM and Jezebel.

Twenty-five Marine snipers positioned them-selves where the FBI snipers had been positioned earlier.

[Scene 132]

Captain Sean got on the radio to another group of Marine soldiers positioned behind Bronx Reynolds.

Captain Sean: "Tango, raise the wall."

About twenty yard away from the rear of the school building, a sophisticated wall, 5cm thick, about the height and length of a tractor trailer and made out of silica tiles, aluminum, and reinforced carbon, was raised. Its purpose was to stop the Jezebel laser beam when it reached the other side of the build-ing.

Along the top of the wall were a number of LED lamps, the type you would see in a football stadium at night. Thus, anyone, including the ter-rorists, would think the wall was just a light stand.

Although the plan was classified, and only the president and the generals knew about the XRBM

Jezebel weapon and how it worked, the plan was simple.

In typical hostage situations, the hostages are always seated, while the captors usually stand on their feet. To identify the captors from the hostages, all the XRainbows have to look for are the figures holding guns. When XRainbows see the captors and their locations inside the building, each non-lethal BM laser marks a target for Jezebel. Each Green Dragon then locks on a target and waits until everyone has a clear shot. All the captors must be taken out at once.

[Scene 133]

[Inside the command post outside Bronx Reynolds]

Captain Sean (on the radio): "All XRainbows, identify your targets."

XRainbow 4: "X-ray radar in progress. Distance is too far. We have to move three feet forward."

Captain Sean: "Roger that. All XRainbows, you are cleared to move three feet forward."

All XRainbows (replying at once): "Moving three feet forward."

[Scene 134]

All XRainbows and Green Dragons repositioned themselves three feet forward.

Captain Sean (on the radio): "All XRainbows, how is your vision?"

XRainbow 8: "Good. Stand by. All radars are still penetrating walls."

XRainbow 2: "I got movement. Figure is carrying a gun."

Captain Sean: "Stay with that figure. What about the hostages? Has anyone seen the hostages?"

XRainbow 2: "Not yet. The figure just entered a room. I can't see him anymore. I have to move a foot forward.

Captain Sean: "All XRainbows, move one foot forward and increase radar power."

All XRainbows and Green Dragons repositioned themselves a foot forward.

XRainbow 5: "I have vision. One, two, three, eight boogies confirmed. There're a lot of figure sitting on the floor."

Captain Sean: "Is there any figure standing up but not holding a gun?"

All XRainbows (replying at once): "Negative."

[Scene 135]

Captain Sean got on the phone with John.

Captain Sean: "How many terrorists are there in the building?"

John: "There are nine confirmed terrorists. I repeat, there are nine terrorists in the building."

Captain Sean: "Roger that."

[Scene 136]

[Outside Bronx Reynolds]

XRainbow 4 (to Captain Sean on the radio): "I see movement in the next room. Someone is doing the salat prayer. He has a gun on his back."

Captain Sean: "Rainbow 4, what the hell is salat?"

XRainbow 4: "Hum . . . It's the standing and kneeling movement performed by Muslims when they're praying."

Captain Sean: "Rainbow 4, stay with him. That's our last target."

[Scene 137]

[Situation Room]

Vice President: "What time is it?"

Secretary of Defense: "6:50 am."

Vice President: "We've got ten minutes before another dead hostage is released."

John called the Marine post outside Bronx Reynolds. Captain Sean answered the phone.

Captain Sean: "Captain Sean."

John: "Captain, what's going on?"

Captain Sean: "Stand by."

Secretary of State: "I don't know what plan you have in progress, but we've got ten minutes remaining before they kill another hostage."

Captain Sean: "Stand by. We are waiting for one more bogie to get in position."

Vice President: "Well, say it to the president. He's listening."

Secretary of Defense: "Where is the president?"

Vice President: "I thought he was sitting behind you."

Collins: "He left for the East Wing some moments ago."

Vice President: "Put him on the phone."

Collins: "I've tried his number twice. He's not answering."

After the Marines had evacuated everyone, including the media, at least four hundred yards away from Bronx Reynolds, no one could see what was happening around the high school. However, I had a radio with me, so I could hear Captain Sean.

[Scene 138]

I arrived on the White House roof. One of the Secret Service snipers on the roof, Agent Nick, turned his face around and was surprised to see me coming.

Agent Nick: "Mr. President, is everything okay, sir?"

Me: "Agent Nick, turn your scope towards Bronx Reynolds. What's going on there?"

Agent Nick: "I can only see approximately a quarter of a mile with my rifle scope, sir. But we have an H59 night vision BEAST, mounted on that Barrett M107 sniper rifle. It can see up to a mile away."

Me: "Let me see it."

[Scene 139]

[Outside Bronx Reynolds]

[6:55am]

XRainbow 8: "Last target is approaching the hostage room."

Captain Sean (speaking to the John on the phone): "I need you to get on the phone with Hammed now. We need him to stand still."

[Scene 140]

[Situation Room]

John: "Copy that. I'm calling him right away."

John called Hammed.

[Scene 141]

[Outside Bronx Reynolds]

XRainbow 8 (speaking to Captain Sean on the radio): "Last target has stopped moving. He's on the phone."

Captain Sean: "Roger that. All XRainbows, transfer digital vision to Green Dragons."

All XRainbows (responding at once): "Vision transferred."

Captain Sean: "Acknowledge. Moving on to BM FF2. All Green Dragons mark your targets."

All Green Dragons (responding at once): "Target marked."

Captain Sean: "One shot, center mass, on my command."

All Green Dragons (responding at once): "One shot, center mass, acknowledged."

Captain Sean: "Activate the red buttons."

All Green Dragons (responding at once): "Jezebel is hot."

Every Marine officer in the vicinity put on their sun shield glasses.

[6:58 am]

Captain Sean: "Get ready to fire . . . and . . . FIRE JEZEBEL."

[Scene 142]

Nine Green Dragons fired the most powerful laser weapon ever created by man into Bronx Reynolds High School. The powerful green laser shot lasted three seconds.

Marines from Bravo Team, split into two groups, stood by at the school entrance, ready to assault the building.

All XRainbows: "All targets are down."

Captain Sean: "Good job, Echo 7. Bravo Team,

you are cleared to assault the building. I want every hostage out here on the floor now. Find and secure the blue hostage first. Be careful. She could be wrapped in explosives."

Bravo Team Leader: "Roger that."

Cataphrase F

"Break every law that is not of God or nature and is not written in the Constitution. The penalty will change your life."

—Teni A.

[Scene 143]

Bravo Team entered the building and secured all the hostages, including the blue hostage.

All the hostages were brought outside. As one Marine explosive expert was deactivating the bomb on Mariah outside the building, the two remaining Bravo Team members in the building ran outside, screaming, "MOVE EVERYONE BACK."

[Scene 144]

Captain Sean (speaking on the radio): "Bravo 8, what the hell is going on?"

Bravo 8: "One boogie is still moving. He was hit in the shoulder. He ran upstairs."

Captain Sean: "Why didn't you go after him and take him out?"

Bravo 8: "He's wearing explosive vest."

Captain Sean: "Son of a bitch!"

XRainbow 4: "I got him. He's on the fifth floor,

behind the wall next to the single window."

Captain Sean: "Green Dragon, can one of you take him out?"

Green Dragon 4: "Negative. He has a height advantage. In order to accurately shoot a target, Jezebel must be at the same height with the target.

Captain Sean: "All snipers, check fifth-floor windows. Does anyone see the terrorist?"

All Marine Snipers: "Negative."

XRainbow 4: "The figure is sitting behind the left wall of the single window facing us."

Captain Sean: "All snipers, does anyone have a .50-caliber rifle?"

Marine Sniper 2: "Negative. We are carrying the MB12D sniper rifle. It's what a hostage situation inside the United States calls for."

Captain Sean: "Goddamn it! A MB12D rifle can't penetrate walls. I need a .50-caliber rifle."

[Scene 145]

[On the White House roof]

Me: "I got one. . . Agent Nick, have any of you ever shot a target at a distance of one mile?"

Agent Nick: "Negative, sir. Only two snipers in history have accomplished a kill at that range: a Canadian army sniper and you, Mr. President . . the Green Viper."

[Short silence]

Me: "Give me the gun."

Agent Nick: "Sir, we only have one round available for the M107 rifle."

Me: "That's all I need."

As I lay on the White House roof, aiming at the

Bronx Reynolds fifth-floor window, Nick approached me.

Agent Nick: "Mr. President, do you want a spotter to join you?"

Me: "The lord is my shepherd. I shall not want . . . He makes me lie down in the green pasture. He led me beside the still waters. He restores my soul.

"He led me to the path of righteousness, for his name sake. Though I walk through the shadow of the battle of death, I'll fear no evil.

"For thou hath with me the rod and the staff. They comfort me. Thou prepared a table before me in the presence of my enemies. Thou anointed my head with oil. My cup runs over.

"Surely, goodness and mercy shall follow me all the days of my life. And I shall dwell in the house of the lord forever….. Kiss my ass."

[BANG ~]

Agent Nick: "Amen."

One shot, one kill. The .50-caliber bullet penetrated the wall a mile away and killed Hammed, setting off the explosive vest he was wearing.

Unless you've done something wrong, a person doesn't give answers unless someone is asking a question. Except for me and the Secret Service snipers on the White House roof that day, no other person knew that a sniper shot was what set off the explosives on the remaining terrorist in the building. No one asked, and no one told.

I had retired my rifle about five years before that day, when I retired from the Marine Corps. But I would pick it up again if I have to. Because, once a Marine, *always a Marine.*

The shield around me isn't hard or soft.
It's just a shield from my own imagination.
I'm always courageous, as if the shield is real.

What has a man who lost his fear in battle got to fear? Even when I'm faced with fire, I'm as brave as water. Gentle in my talk, but loud in my actions. I do to others as I would do to myself.

When others asked for peace, they gave me a rifle. When everyone asked for riches, I just wanted the simple things in life: love, liberty, and happiness. *Maybe a nice little old country Cadillac, if life is so kind.* If not, I'll accept the rodeo and move on. My approach to life is simple: live it or leave it. And until the day my strength fades away, the day the lion can no longer hunt, the day my eyelids close and my gray hair falls out, I'll continue to fight the fight of freedom and sing the song of hope. Because, once a Marine, *always a Marine.*

[Scene 146]

[Inside command post outside Bronx Reynolds]

Captain Sean (speaking to the marine general): "General, the situation is resolved. Last target is down. All hostages are secured."

Marine General: "Where is Mariah?"

Captain Sean: "She's on a Marine helicopter heading for the White House as we speak. Sir, should I hand the scene over to the FBI?"

Marine General: "Yes, you can. You are cleared to leave. Thanks, Captain."

Captain Sean: "Always at your command, sir."

[Scene 147]

[The next day at the US Capitol]

Press members were questioning the White House press secretary.

Reporter: "Is it true that the president spoke to the terrorist? And, Mr. Secretary, is it true that the US government attempted to offer the terrorists a deal in exchange for the hostages?"

Press Secretary: "The president never spoke to any of the terrorists, and the United States government does not negotiate with terrorists. The president did what was necessary to save Americans and defend our Constitution."

[9:22 am]

As the next reporter was about to ask a question, I entered the room and took over from the press secretary.

Female Reporter: "Mr. President, why did you de

ploy the military to resolve a hostage situation inside the United States?"

Me: "The situation appeared to everyone to be a hostage situation, but in fact, it was more than a hostage situation. It was an act of war. I did what I have to do to protect Americans and defend the United States Constitution."

Second Female Reporter: "Mr. President, there are rumors that the main reason why you deployed the military was because your daughter was among the hostages. The question I have for you is, would you have done the same thing you did yesterday if Mariah hadn't been among the hostages?"

Me: "I did. Maybe you have forgotten, but I will remind you."

I took off my shirt and pointed to the gunshot wounds on my body. As I pointed at each scar, I described how I got it.

Me: "Operation Green Apple, 1995. I was shot here in my abdomen when I was trying to rescue an American hostage. That hostage wasn't my daughter.   "Operation ASCAP, 1996. I took a bullet here in my shoulder for two American hostages. None of them was my daughter.

"Operation Red November, 1997. I received several bits of shrapnel to my back after I covered a fellow Marine officer from a grenade explosion. That Marine officer was just another American, not any of my relatives.

"So, ask me one more time if I would do what I did yesterday if my Mariah hadn't been among the hostages, and I'll tell you the story of my grandfather, an Army Ranger who died in Vietnam during World War ll.

"Ask me again, and I'll tell you the story of my nephew, one of the troops I deployed to Syria the second week I became president.

"Ask me again if the United States president will move heaven and earth to defend its citizen, and I'll show you the scars of Hiroshima and Nagasaki.

"Ask me the question again, and I'll tell you, you are not an American.

"After it's all said and done, if this building suddenly caught fire, there're two groups of people in this room: the ones who will run outside and the ones who will run inside to make sure everyone is safe before they run out. I know which group I belong to. Which group do you belong to?"

A complete silence filled the room. I put back on my shirt.

Me: "The question before us today shouldn't be about my patriotism or my service to the nation. History has shown that the president is more likely to start World War III because a terrorist mistakenly stepped on an American spider. The question we should be asking is, how ready are we when disaster strikes?

"With the push of a button, I can send a missile to destroy a target anywhere in the world. But where is the quick button to press if I need to send urgent help to Americans in times of trouble?

"Do we have in place a solid plan, and can we respond in minutes with enough gas masks if a terrorist attacked us today with a deadly gas weapon?

"Do we have ready, and can we respond in minutes, with the best drills if another miner gets stuck in a hole today?

"Do we have any solid rescue plan, and can we respond in minutes, if Hurricane Katrina happens again today?

"If any of our mighty submarines roaming the oceans sink as we speak, is there any solid plan in place to respond within minutes to save our submariners wherever they are in the depths of the ocean?

"Do we have any plan ready to save and rescue millions of Americans if disaster strikes in a manner we've never seen before?

"These are the questions we should be asking. For I say to you that a nation's greatness isn't complete until it has the power to save as much as it has the power to destroy.

When I became president of the United States, I was assigned a presidential black box. The box contains the power to authorize a nuclear attack in minutes while away from a fixed point.
That box was useless on 9/11. And again, it was useless yesterday.

"Therefore, today, I, Neil Kenneth Bull, president of the United States of America, by virtue of the power in me vested as commander in chief of the armed forces to defend the Constitution of the Unites States and protect its citizens at home and abroad, I demand that Congress deliver to me within one hundred days another presidential brief-case containing a button that can release help to Americans in times war, disaster, or public danger. This must be a release of all the United States government's resources, including military forces and technologies, wherever it may be stored on earth or outside the earth, in secret or in open, without any delay or hindrance.

"These two presidential boxes containing the power to save and destroy shall follow me every-where I go, at home and abroad, until I'm no longer president of the United States. Thank you."

[Scene 148]

What was left of the Bronx Reynolds building would later be demolished and recreated into a memorial. The words on the marble read:

I pledge allegiance to the flag of the United States and to the republic for which it stands, one nation under God, indivisible, with liberty and justice for all.
    Dedicated to those who died at Bronx Reynolds High School on June 28, most especially, the Marine soldier who gave his life to save others. Your memories will forever live in our hearts.

[Scene 149]

[July 4, a week after the hostage incident]

[Independence Day ceremony at the White House]

[Inside the White House]

Me (speaking from the living room): "Guys, I'm ready when you are."

Chelsea (replying from the bedroom): "Hold on. Let me finish my makeup."

Me: "Not again. The last time I waited, the Independence Day celebration was over before we arrived. Guys, let's go. Your mum will join us outside when she's finished."

Mariah: "Dad, can I ask for something?"

Me: "Nope. No fireworks. You don't even have to ask. If it's fireworks, the answer is no. This is your first time coming out since that thing at your school happened. The rest of your classmates are waiting outside."

Mariah: "Not fireworks, Dad, I just want to ask if I can sing the national anthem before the celebrities start performing."

[Short silence]

Me: "I'll think about it."

[Last Scene, 150]

[Outside the White House]

Me (speaking to White House guests)**:** "Hello, everyone. Happy independence Day.

"I want to welcome all of you to the White House. It's great to have you here with us for the Independence Day celebration. Before we continue, I know you all remember what happened last week at Bronx Reynolds High School. Some of those involved in the situation are here today to celebrate with us.

"To those who lost their lives during the incident, let's observe a moment of silence to honor them."

[A moment silence]

Me: "Before we start the fireworks and introduce the celebrities we have for you today, on behalf of everyone who took part in the rescue mission last week, Mariah would like to show her appreciation by singing the national anthem of the United States of America. Mariah . . ."

Mariah wore a silver silk dress. With slight tears rolling down her cheeks, she took the microphone.

Mariah: "Oh say can you see, by the dawn's early light, What so proudly we hailed at the twilight's last gleaming? Whose broad stripes and bright stars, through the perilous fight'
O'er the ramparts we watched were so gallantly streaming?
And the rocket's red glare, the bombs bursting in air,
Gave proof through the night that our flag was still there.
Oh, say does that star-spangled banner yet wave,
O'er the land of the freeeeeeeeeeeeeeeeeeee and the home of the brave?"

[~Fireworks bursting in air~]

THE END .